Falling for You

Peyton Corners

Solara Gordon

Published by THE EARTH MOVED, LLC, 2021.

FALLING FOR YOU

First edition. September 4, 2021.

ISBN: 978-1737305927

Written by Solara Gordon.

Also by Solara Gordon

Cascade Bay
Love Reborn

Peyton Corners
Falling for You

Standalone
A Heart's Desire
To Love You Again
To Love You Again

Watch for more at https://solaragordon.com/.

There's a saying a picture is worth a thousand words. The picture can spark intrigue, an idea, and questions all leading to the two people in the picture telling you their story. Drake and Sara popped into my mind and heart igniting a story of second chances at love and romance. A unique experience and setting that came alive as I wrote their story. Peyton Corners is a place where people find new beginnings, second chances at love and romance. I'm sure Peyton Corners has more stories waiting to be told. Magic occurs when my characters share their story and journey with me.

Thank you to my street team and readers group, Solara's Glamorous Stars. You keep me intrigued and engaged with your encouragement and support. A special thank you goes to the following beta readers: Christine Travis, Denise Leitch-Gaff, Monique Coker, Christine Heydt, and Jo BookLover. Each of you helped enrich and add depth to Drake and Sara's love story.

CHAPTER ONE

Thursday Night

T Across the street, the neighbor's holiday lights twinkled and blinked, accenting the windblown snow dancing in the air. Swirls of white crystalline flakes billowed up and down before settling on the others already covering the yard. Sara Johnston dropped the curtain, stepping away from the front window. Winter had arrived like the holidays. This year was different. *Boy, was it different.*

A new job, a new town, and a new neighbor. Drake McCallister filled out a pair of jeans nicer than any of her fantasies ever came up with. The man had an awesome trunk to quote her best friend, Lindsay. Sara smiled as Lindsay's qualifying additional statement came to mind. Drake's ass couldn't compare with Lindsay's husband's. Lindsay's husband, Michael, had a lot of women lusting after him. A fireman's physique sparked female hormones, igniting a two-alarm fire that refused to be put out.

Michael's cousin Drake had moved into the house behind hers almost two months ago. The few times he'd spoken to her, Sara hadn't said much. Getting to know her neighbor hadn't worked before now. She had to get to know him since he was her so-called blind date for the fire station's holiday fundraiser. Dinner, dancing and a silent auction helped raise funds for Peyton Corners' new fire station and the new urgent care center.

Sara flopped down on the couch, sighing. Two days and nights to get to know Drake. He was upstairs in her guest bath showering. The pipes in his house were frozen thanks to no heat and downed electrical wires. Living at the edge of town had its difficulties. This blasted snow and windstorm was a downer for sure. Not really per Lindsay. Living at the end of a cul-de-sac offered her some protection from the wind and drifting snow.

Drake, naked, wet and soapy. . . upstairs in her house. Close to her bedroom. . .and—Oh hell, she had to get her mind off stripping him naked and having her way with him. Thoughts of him doing the same to her fueled a few moments of delicious images. Mutual desire, interest, and doing something about it gave her libido ideas to mull over. Tonight's dreams were sure to be much different from her last two.

The shower shut off. Sara glanced up. Her signal, time to set the table. She'd run to the grocery before the storm hit. Between what Drake had brought over and what she had, they were set. The pork roast in the crockpot needed shredding and a bit more barbecue sauce to give it a smoldering tang. Pulled pork sandwiches, homemade potato chips, and mulled wine was the main course. Dessert, thanks to Drake making sure the fireplace's wood bin was full, was smores with more mulled wine or herbal tea.

"Ok, Sara," she began, standing. "Get your thoughts out of the man's pants and on food."

Sara grinned as she walked into the kitchen. If anyone had told her she'd be spending a cold, snowy Thursday night with one of the hottest men she knew, she'd have told them they were nuts. Absolutely bonkers. Then sometimes, prayers were answered. Hers had been to bring a man into her life she could respect, honor and wanted to have a relationship with. The wind whistled outside the kitchen window, rattling the grate on the exterior screen door. Was this the signal Drake was the one?

She poured half of the open bottle of red rose wine into a saucepan and set it on the stove on a low burner after adding mulling spices. Slow steady heat with occasional stirring would mix the wine and the spices together. Cinnamon, allspice, and nutmeg greeted her as she sniffed. She and Drake had tasted the wine before allowing it to breathe and warm. The tang from the cherries, red wood aging, and white grapes tantalized her taste buds. Peyton Corners' main vintner had come through again according to Drake.

The roast sat cooling on a platter close to the crockpot. A bowl containing her grandmother's blue ribbon-winning barbecue sauce sat next to it. Pieces of the roast hung off it, ready to drop onto the platter. A few slices and shreds would turn it into a pile ready to mix with the sauce. Buns toasted in the toaster. The chips she made earlier were in a bowl on the table. Drake had joked about needing a roll of paper towels to keep from dripping sauce all over after he tasted her grandmother's sauce. Sara was sure her grandmother never thought of her sauce as an enticing prelude to scintillating conversation or even a steamy one. Drake had winked and said five words before he rushed upstairs to shower. Food and what a night.

Sara shredded the last pieces of the roast, added it to the sauce bowl and stirred. Drake couldn't mean more than a good meal, maybe a movie or two, and a fire in the fireplace. Could he? Confidence—willpower and fortitude. She knew she could, she would and had the will to not embarrass herself. After all, it wasn't like she would sit there drooling while Drake ate dinner or talked with her. He was eye candy for sure. Candy she enjoyed immensely since he returned with a packed duffle bag and his basket of dirty clothes, cussing about his electric being out. Being a good neighbor had its perks.

She stirred the pork and sauce one more time. As she walked toward the table, she noted the steam rising from the pan warming the wine. She clicked the burner off and set the pan on the opposite cool burner. The spices and wine needed to mull for another five to ten minutes.

How soon would Drake be ready to eat? What happened then? Would a simple line like tell me about yourself seem too corny a conversation starter?

Drake hung his damp towel over the towel rack close to the tub shower combination. Today had been one of those days. Two flat tires on his truck before he even left for work. An hour and half late due to waiting for the tow truck. Five hundred dollars later, his credit card smoked closer to its limit after he paid for two new tires and the labor to put them on. Then there was work. His long weekend turned into a double shift because his relief was stranded across country due to the airport closure and the snowstorm raging outside. Jeff, his shift relief partner, had called twice, apologizing profusely and offering to work a double for him once he got back. He had turned Jeff down. Going to your little sister's wedding was important. Family mattered when you had some.

Drake sighed. He couldn't change his past. His parents did the best they could for him and his siblings. His grandparents took over when his parents passed. So what if he had to work through Christmas. It was better than sitting home alone. For now, he wasn't alone. Sara waited for him. Company. Good food and—the one woman that sparked his interest. Quiet and unobtrusive. She lent a hand at community events. Helped at the volunteer fire department fundraisers. Even served a term on the county board of directors. How did he signal his interest?

He glanced in the mirror. "First, I gotta put some clothes on." He grinned, combing his fingers through his hair. He quickly pulled on his briefs and t-shirt. He glanced around the bathroom. Crap, he'd left his jeans in on the bed. He cracked the door open, peered out, hoping Sara wasn't coming up the stairs as he darted out of the bathroom.

Halfway to his room, two loud barks sounded. Drake stopped, glaring at the guard in front of the bedroom door. Two-tone tan, floppy ears and a stubby tail that moved fast enough to wiggle its hind end. McGee, Sara's dachshund, barked again.

"Shhh, McGee!" Drake chastised. "I'll pet you after I get dressed."

McGee moved closer to him, wiggling, and whining. Drake crouched down, held his hand out. McGee sniffed his hand, wiggled more, and flopped down in front of him.

"All right, a couple of pets. Then I gotta get dressed." Drake stroked McGee twice and stood up. Two steps away from McGee, he started barking again. Drake rolled his eyes, shook his head, and trotted toward the bedroom door.

"Drake, is something wrong with McGee?" Sara called out.

If he stopped to answer, Sara would see him in his underwear. Not that that was a bad thing. It wasn't time for it. Great impression saved for better timing like when they were passionately making out and pulling each other's clothes off. Now wasn't that time. Drake grabbed the bedroom doorknob and turned it.

McGee kept barking and racing around him. Two more steps and. . . .

"McGee, quiet," Sara called. "I'm coming."

Drake flung the door open, sending it banging against the wall. He ducked behind it as he glanced over his shoulder. Sara was halfway up the stairs.

McGee followed him into the bedroom, whining and barking. Drake grabbed his jeans off the bed, shook them out, and inserted his foot into one leg. Short and quick to pull em on right? No such luck. McGee latched on to the leg close to him, growling and shaking it.

"Look you little shit, let go of my pants." Drake tugged. McGee growled and shook more. "I said let go!"

"McGee! Those are Drake's pants. Not your play toy!" Sara's voice echoed off the door deep into the room. Silence followed.

How red could a grown man flush? Did embarrassment stop once you got past your teens? Drake let go of his jeans, dropped onto the bed, and sighed. Talk about getting caught with your pants down. At least he wasn't buckass naked like the time his Dad and his girlfriend's dad almost caught him and his girlfriend playing strip spin the bottle in the hayloft.

"Uh, sorry?' He looked up, unsure how to meet Sara's gaze. At least he didn't have a hard-on.

Sara smiled at him and winked. "Nothing to be sorry about. My nephews got McGee started on denim toys. It used to be squeaky toys."

Drake forced a chuckle. "Sounds like my niece's cat. Had to hide anything with catnip. The cat would shred boxes, toys and even plastic bags to get at the stuff."

"McGee, come," Sara called, turning around. McGee let go of the jeans, yipped and trotted over to Sara.

'Thanks. I'll be down in a few." Drake leaned down, reaching for his jeans.

"Sure. Dinner is ready. So am I. . ." Sara began, walking away, not finishing her thought.

Drake quickly pulled on his jeans, and threaded his belt through the belt loops. He didn't know if he needed to apologize more or be prepared to walk around the invisible elephant in the room the size of a miniature dachshund he decided to nickname piss ant McGee. Though he'd never call him that out loud.

He pulled on a plain-colored t-shirt, tucked it into his jeans, and slipped his feet into his driving moccasins. As he started down the stairs, he wasn't sure he'd broken the ice, slipped on or sat on it and froze a certain part of his anatomy. One thing he knew for certain, dinner and the rest of his stay were off to one hell of a start.

CHAPTER TWO

Sara reached the bottom of the stairs, glanced behind her and gave up suppressing her grin. She'd gotten an eye full. A sight she hadn't expected to see. Lindsay was right. Firefighters had one hell of a physique. Drake rippled in *all* the right places. Strong muscular legs and arms, and he had male curves. His abs and pecs spoke of his strength and exercise.

Now she had to get her mind back on dinner. Otherwise, she'd be standing right where she was when Drake came down the stairs. McGee had run into the kitchen and came back out barking. He wanted dinner, pets, and his half hour of attention after he made his last potty run outside. Nights like tonight, cold and snowy, made her glad she had chosen the place with the fenced in yard. She could let McGee out. Watch him as she set the table.

Sara walked to the back door and opened it part way. "McGee, come. Go outside."

McGee ran up to the door, sniffed, and turned around. Sara reached down and grabbed his collar as he started past her. "No, you're going out. Cold or not. You can be fast. I know it."

Sara opened the door, shivering slightly as the wind buffeted the door. She set McGee down outside the door and pulled it to her. McGee scooted back toward the door, nuzzling the open space with his nose, trying to push the door open more. Sara leaned down, gently pushed him back, and closed the door. Yips and barks sounded. She turned away, moving out of sight of the window. McGee would fuss a bit more then make a bee line for his favorite pee corner near the back corner adjacent to the neighbor's yard. Their boxer, Boris, often marked his corner right along with McGee. The two exchanged barks and short growls from time to time. Perhaps they were greeting each other or bragging.

She took plates out of the cabinet near the sink, set them on the table along with napkins and utensils. In the center of the table, she put the bowl of shredded barbecue pork, the plate with warmed buns next to it, and a bowl filled with homemade chips next to them. As she walked back into the kitchen, McGee started barking at the door. She looked out the kitchen window. Evidence of McGee's potty run stood out against the stark whiteness of the latest snowfall. Sara stood behind the door and opened it. McGee bolted in, rushing past her making a dead beeline for the living room.

Sara quickly shut and locked the door. "Stop, McGee!" She ran right behind the little culprit. "McGee, come here!"

He jumped up on the couch, ran across it, and dived off it on to the wingback chair near the front window and off the chair heading for the stairs. Wet feet, wet fur, and mud tracks left nothing to imagine. If she didn't corner McGee, her bed or Drake's, possibly both were going to need clean sheets. Sara started up the stairs just as McGee reached the middle step. "McGee, sit. Stay."

McGee turned, looked at her, shook from his head to his tail, and ignored her. He barked and took off up the rest of the steps.

Drake turned back to his bedroom door, grabbed it, and pulled it shut. He didn't stop to ask how he could help. He went into help mode. He quickened his pace, pausing long enough to grab his towel out of the bathroom. He moved close to the top of the stairs and crouched, holding the towel out in front of him. He focused on one thing and one thing only. The sight of Sara bounding up the stairs wasn't a bad sight. One thing mattered, capturing a two-tone menace hell bent on diving under or on a bed. McGee was about to find out how quick a firefighter's reflexes were.

"Come here, McGee," Drake called. "I'll protect you."

He shook the towel and called McGee again. Two steps down McGee halted, tilted his head from side to side, and barked. His tail wagged each time Drake said his name.

A few steps behind McGee, Sara stood still. Drake glanced up, caught her gaze, nodded, and lowered the towel some. "Come on, McGee. That snow and mud gotta be cold and wet. Once you're dry, I bet there might be a treat for you."

Drake lowered the towel more, pooling it on the floor in front of him. He let go of one corner of the towel and reached out toward McGee, hoping he distracted him. McGee spun around barked at Sara and made a beeline straight for her. "Look out Sara. Muddy dog coming through."

"No, McGee," Sara called out, moving up a step. "Stay."

Drake grabbed up the towel and started down the steps. McGee sped past him and Sara, bolting down the hall toward Sara's bedroom.

"Clever mutt," Drake muttered, carefully turning around, ready to give chase.

"Sometimes too clever for his own good," Sara said right behind him. "He's headed for my room. Probably the clothes basket by my bed too."

"This isn't an issue?" Drake asked, pausing at the top of the stairs.

"Basket is full of towels that need washing." Sara trotted past him, adding, "If McGee gets in my bed, that's something else."

Drake shook his head and quickened his pace.

Sara slowed her pace as she reached her bedroom doorway. McGee was nowhere in sight. She'd glanced in her bathroom as she passed the open door. There were two places McGee liked to hide in the bathroom. The space between the toilet and the wall close to the shower stall and under the sink if he could get the cabinet doors open. She made sure the cabinet doors were latched before she went downstairs this morning. McGee had been with her up until he decided to investigate Drake and snuck upstairs while he was in the shower. That left two places the mischievous culprit could be. In the middle of her bed, rolling around trying to dry off and burrow his way under her comforter or in the basket of dirty towels she'd forgotten to put in the washer.

Drake came up behind her. "Something wrong?"

She held up her hand, shaking her head. "No and yes. McGee is playing hide and seek. Muddy wet hide and seek. Getting up my nerve to check on his last two hiding places."

"How can I help?" Drake put his hand on her shoulder.

Sara flexed her fingers. Warmth flowed off Drake's palm down over her shoulder and pooled deep within her cleavage, spilling out across her nipples. She looked down. Taut and pebbling more, soon there be no mistaking how Drake's touch affected her. She reached up patted Drake's hand and slightly turned. "Try to keep McGee from escaping. If he's in the dirty towels, I can grab him and dry him off. My bed..."

She didn't say more. Changing the sheets would take twenty minutes and delay dinner. Tucking the corners in on the flat sheets she used as bottom sheets wasn't easy. Asking Drake to help with that—was a bit more personal and intimate than she—she had to change where her thoughts were going. It wasn't like Drake was interested in her or indicated even a sexual attraction. If she let her mind roam much more, she'd be flushed, possibly blushing and her nipples would be showing for sure.

"Let me go in first?" Drake asked. "It might roust McGee out."

Sara snorted. "We want to capture him not play hunt down McGee until he tires out."

"He does have a lot of energy." Drake moved up beside her.

"He has his moments. I'll go in first." Sara started to enter her bedroom. "You block the doorway so he can't make good on his escape."

"Right behind you." Drake stepped back, adding, "I'll help give him a bath and dry him off."

"Thanks. Maybe after dinner." Sara looked toward her bed as she moved into her room, sighing. There in the middle of her bed sat the muddy, wet, two-tone tail wagging pain. Somehow, McGee managed to tip the laundry basket by the bed upside down allowing him to jump up on the bed. Muddy paw prints stood out against the pale yellow sheets and beige comforter. Wet splotches littered her pillows and nightgown as if McGee had rolled back and forth on them several times. She let out a deep sigh and reached for one of the towels on the floor closest to her.

"McGee you scamp." She started toward the bed. McGee's tail wagged faster.

Drake pressed his lips together. There was a humorous side to this. How a four-legged rascal could get the better of he and Sara baffled him. The whole thing reminded him of watching his three and four-year-old nephews who loved to strip off their clothes and streak through the yard naked during the summer after playing in their wading pool. Chasing them down with towels to dry them off had become a regular game. McGee reminded him of Jason and Alexander. Reasoning with a toddler or a determined canine wasn't easy or made sense.

"I think a b-a-t-h soon is probably a good idea, yes?" Drake walked into the bedroom and closed the door behind him.

"Maybe. We've got to catch him first." Sara stretched the towel out in front of her like he had. She moved close to the bed. McGee started for the opposite side.

Drake leaned down grabbed the laundry basket and ran around the foot of the bed. As he got near the other side of the bed, he turned the basket over and waited. McGee ran straight toward him, picking up speed the closer he got. Drake held the basket up with both hands and leaned forward. One-McGee tried to turn around. Two-Drake stretched his arms out. Three-Perfect snare. McGee zip. Drake full score. McGee tried to tip the basket over. No luck. Drake had put his hand on top of the basket. "Give it up, dude. You're getting a warm bath."

"Thank you. I've got a couple of towels we can use to dry him off for now." Sara sat down on the foot of the bed.

"Let's get the bath done. I have a feeling he's going to try to get under the bed if we don't." Drake started to lift the basket. "I'll help you change the bed after dinner, okay?"

Sara nodded as she grabbed McGee by his collar. "Your help is appreciated." She walked out of the bedroom, holding a squirming McGee tight to her.

Drake picked up the towels Sara had tossed on the bed before she sat down. He smiled watching Sara walk away. Why was she flushed? Blushing? Nice bust and nipples. Bathing McGee wasn't going to leave space to daydream. McGee demanded full on attention. Drake reached down and tugged on the crotch of his jeans. Things were a bit warm around his balls and cock.

CHAPTER THREE

Sara didn't put McGee down until she was in her bathroom. She set him in the soaker tub opposite the shower stall. He couldn't easily get out. She took off his collar and laid it on the edge of the tub. McGee whined and nuzzled her hand. "You aren't sorry. You're getting a bath. Stop fussing. You brought this on rolling in the snow and mud."

McGee sat down, looked up at her, with his sad doggy eyes look. Sara snickered. "Not buying that look either dude. Keep it up and you'll find yourself with no bedtime treat."

McGee yipped and rolled on his back. Sara shook her head as she turned on the water, testing its temperature.

"Got a personality all his own," Drake offered entering the bathroom. "What can I help with?"

"There's a bottle of dog shampoo in the cabinet under the counter. Make sure you latch the door. That's one of his prime hiding places." Sara glanced over her shoulder. She was getting an eye full. Drake bent over with his jeans outlining the curves of his well-formed ass and if he were nude, she'd have a great view of his cock and balls.

"Sara," Drake said. "Hey Sara is this what you're looking for?"

Sara ducked her head, blinked and looked up at what Drake held out to her. Crap! Drake had caught her ogling him. He smiled and winked as she reached for the shampoo he held. "That's it. Thanks."

"Soap 'em twice?"

"No, once is enough. Just need more than one towel or he'll shake water everywhere." Sara poured a small amount of shampoo into her hand, stuck it under the water flowing out of the tub spigot, and started working the latter into McGee's coat. She used her other hand to add water to the soapy mixture.

"I brought two more with me. I shut your bedroom door, too." Drake perched on the edge of the tub. "Would a cup or glass help with rinsing him? There's one on the back of the sink."

"Focused on making sure McGee didn't escape. I forgot the glass. Sure do need it." She took the glass from Drake. His fingers brushed hers. She swore sparks jumped from him to her. Gripping the glass tight, she focused on soaping and rinsing McGee. Five minutes later, McGee was trying to make good his escape by standing on his hind legs and jumping up on the edge of the tub.

Drake grabbed one of the towels close to him and flung it over McGee. "Time to dry you off. Be good and you might get a treat." Drake leaned down into the tub. McGee started tussling under the towel, squirming away from Drake. "Hold still, McGee."

Sara stood up. "Be careful, you'll..." Drake turned to glance at Sara. Soap slicked his hand as he reached for the side of the tub trying to steady himself as he grappled with a towel covered McGee.

"Drake, grab my hand." Sara held her hand out to him.

Drake clasped Sara's hand and let go of McGee. Heat seared across his palm, over his fingers and up his arm. The tighter he gripped Sara's hand the hotter the sizzle got. It was like jagged bursts of warmth poured off her and ignited his own desire until it swamped him overflowing deep into his midsection. He up righted himself and let go. He quickly looked at his hand and at Sara. She was busy drying McGee. She had felt the heat too right? How could she not?

"Are you okay?" Sara moved closer to him.

"You didn't feel it?" Drake looked at his hand again. No color changes. He glanced at Sara. She was flushed some. She had to have felt it.

"Feel what? Your soapy wet hand?" Sara moved back a step.

"The heat flashing off us. The sparks. You didn't see them?" Drake held his hand up. "Tell me why you're flushed again?"

As if on cue, McGee barked and tried to escape the tub. Drake shot McGee the best sideways evil look he could while trying to figure out how to keep the conversation going. Something was happening between Sara and him. "Come on, Sara. Talk to me. I'll help you dry McGee. There's something going on between us."

Sara's gaze met his for a split second and she looked away. "Well, maybe I noticed something. Are you saying you did?"

Drake inhaled and exhaled slowly. Was Sara playing aloof or her reaction to him bothered her? Michael and Lindsay had advised him to get to know whoever he got paired up with for the community fund raising dance. There were a couple of women who flirted with him. None of them intrigued him like Sara did. One prior girlfriend had set his chemistry off like this in his teens. This was the reaction his grandfather talked about when he said his late wife put the pizazz and zing in every touch and kiss they shared. Grandpa told him when he found the woman who got him hot, bothered and sparked, she was the one for him. The connection with Sara certainly was setting more than a few sparks off.

"I sure did. Twice." Drake leaned down, wrapped the towel around McGee, and lifted him out of the tub. He set McGee on the counter and began toweling him off. "I'd like to talk about it."

Sara held out another towel. "How about we talk as we eat?"

Drake took the other towel and nodded. "We finish with McGee first."

"Yes. I'll toss the other towel on the couch. He'll probably curl up on it and sleep." Sara held up her crossed fingers.

Drake grinned. "Understood."

Ten minutes later, McGee scampered down the stairs as if he was escaping. Sara followed close behind him, towel flung over her shoulder, and Drake following her. Taming McGee down was nothing to calming the butterflies fluttering in multiple directions in her stomach. Picking a neutral ice breaking conversation starter wasn't happening. Instead, the stage lights were on bright and focused on her and Drake center stage.

"I'll warm up the pork and buns." Sara paused as she reached the bottom of the stairs. "Do you mind starting a small fire in the fireplace? I thought we might toast marshmallows and make smores for dessert.""

"Sure. I'll keep an eye on it while we eat. It'll have burned down enough we can toast marshmallows without setting them on fire." Drake followed her into the kitchen. "I'll dowse the ashes in the ash bucket and set it outside away from the house before we go to bed."

"Thank you." Sara picked up the pork and buns off the table. "It'll take a few moments to heat this up."

She put the bowl of shredded pork in the microwave and turned it on. She turned around and faced Drake. "I guess you know I'm attracted to you."

Drake smiled. "I can say the same. We got chemistry."

"Appears so. How do you feel about this?" Sara leaned against the counter.

"I think it's nice. I like it. How about you?" Drake took a step toward her.

"It's different." The microwave timer rang. She took the steaming bowl out and put the buns into warm. "I mean we're here. Sorta forced together and yet set up if you add the dance to the mix."

"Yeah. How do you feel here?" Drake touched her close to her heart. Could he feel her pulse race? The heat that ignited even with his slight touch?

"Am I comfortable with our attraction?" Her gaze didn't leave Drake's.

"Yes. You're safe." Drake leaned closer and whispered. "I'm big on consent and getting to know each other."

"Thank you. I appreciate knowing that. You're safe too." Sara winked and turned around.

Drake chuckled. "Good to know. For now, let's eat and have our first date discussion."

Sara chortled, holding the heated bowl out to Drake. "Sounds like a plan considering we're in a situation that most people don't have until they've dated for a while."

"True. Staying over on the first date doesn't happen often." Drake took the bowl and headed toward the table. He added as he walked away, "We might have a better discussion than if we were out in public. No one to interrupt us. McGee is asleep."

"I owe you an apology. McGee—" Sara didn't say more. Drake had turned back toward her with his hand up.

"McGee is McGee. He's inquisitive. A pain. Loves to have fun. And he's a dog. An intelligent dog." Drake placed the bowl on the table. "He had us chasing him like he wanted."

"He sure did." Sara took the buns out of the microwave. "Thanks for understanding."

Drake grinned as he walked back toward her. "He wanted attention. We gave it to him. Now we can pay attention to each other. Where are your wine glasses? I'll pour the wine."

"Cabinet to the left of the sink. I hope the wine isn't over spiced." She set the buns on the table, pulled out a chair and sat down.

"If it is, we add some from the open bottle. Half a glass is fine for me. You?" Drake set two glasses on the counter.

"Half for me, too." Sara placed two buns on each plate and spooned pork and sauce on to them. "Let's eat. While I do the dishes, you can start the fire."

"I'll help clean up too. " Drake placed the half-full glasses on the table. "Then I'll start the fire."

Sara handed Drake his plate with a sandwich and a handful of chips. Drake picked up his sandwich and took a bite. He glanced at Sara who watched him.

"I have a question. Don't want to catch you off guard, but I'm getting you hot and bothered, right?" Sara picked up her sandwich and took a bite.

Drake pressed his lips tighter together. He couldn't easily swallow. Sara didn't want to catch him off-guard. She asked a hot topic question when he had a mouthful. He set his sandwich down, continued chewing, and slowly swallowed. He sipped his wine and laid his hands on the table. "Touché. You imp."

Sara pointed at herself and shrugged. Drake smirked, shaking his head. "Not a bad imp. I can see how you and McGee get along so well."

Sara winked at him as she wiped her mouth. "A friend said McGee and I were a couple of rascals. He makes me laugh."

"Good." Drake raised his wine glass. "Now as to you getting me hot and bothered. Oh, yeah. Raise my temperature in all the right places. Now my turn to ask a question."

Sara picked up her wine glass, clinked it softly against Drake's and said, "Maybe I won't blush this time."

Drake set his glass down and snickered. "I'll wait until you're done sipping your wine. Gives me time to think of a good one. A sure to make you blush one."

Should she glance away? Let him know his banter and touches lit a fire deep inside her? Left her thinking about what kind of lover he was? Oh, how hot and steamy had this conversation and her thoughts gotten.

Drake laid his hands on the table and leaned forward. "My question is a two-parter. Why are you flushing again? Can you deny I get you hot and bothered?"

Sara sipped more of her wine. She held her glass up. "Might be the wine. Then again. . . ."

CHAPTER FOUR

"Then again what?" Drake asked, leaning back in his chair. Sara flushed so nicely. Down the sides of her neck, across what he could see of her shoulders and the top of her cleavage. Did she flush all the way down and over her breasts to her nipples? He slid his hand off the table. He reached part way down on his thigh and tugged his jeans. His cock and balls were demanding attention. He didn't want the conversation to stop too quickly. Talk about some hot and heavy duty flirting!

Sara pointed at him, grinned, and spoke. "The extra is you do turn me on. Eye candy is worth the enjoyment. Have I answered your question?"

Drake held his hand up. "High five, honey. High five! Great response. Oh yeah you answered my question for sure."

"Good. Let's finish eating before our food gets cold." Sara picked up her sandwich and went back to eating.

"Agreed." Drake scooped up shredded pork and sauce with his chips. "Good food. Good company."

Sara nodded and kept eating. Drake finished his sandwich and pushed back from the table. "I'll get the fire started. By the time we're done eating, it should be burned down enough to bank the coals."

He didn't look back as he walked away from the table. He could sense Sara watching him. Enjoying her eye candy. Bursts of heat leaped out of his groin up into his heart, adding to the growing feeling he couldn't label. He hadn't enjoyed this much banter and flirting in a long time. A year plus. His last relationship had mutually dissolved. She accepted a full time teaching position at a university in Utah. He wasn't ready to move away from his grandparents until last year when they moved to their retirement home in Las Vegas.

"How can I help?" Sara asked getting up from the table.

"I need matches, kindling, some wadded up paper to get the fire started. A few larger pieces of kindling will help keep the fire burning for a bit before it starts to burn down." Drake opened the fireplace door, picked up the poker, and stirred the ash residue from a prior fire. "Hand me the ash bucket, please."

Sara placed the ash bucket close to the edge of the hearth next to Drake. "I'll get the matches and paper. Be right back."

Drake nodded, not looking up to see if Sara saw. He laid the poker aside, picked up the broom, shovel dustpan, and cleaned out the old ashes and residue from a prior fire. As he placed the tools back on the fireplace tool stand, he noted where Sara was. She was still in the kitchen. "Newspaper is the best for starting the fire. No color print if possible."

"You're in luck," she called out. "Missed the recycle truck. Got two days' worth of paper. How much do you need?"

"A half dozen wadded sheets will do. Do you have fire place matches?" Drake placed small pieces of kindling in the center of the fireplace grate, leaving spaces to insert the paper wads.

"Yes. I've got them." Sara came up beside him as he straightened. She held out the long container of fireplace matches. In her other hand was several wads of newspaper. "If you need more let me know."

Five minutes later a bright yellow and blue flame ignited the paper and part of the kindling. Drake closed the fireplace door and moved back. "My turn to help you with kitchen clean up and putting the food away."

"I appreciate it. Team work makes clean up quick and easy." Sara started toward the kitchen. "Do you prefer to wash or dry?"

Drake chuckled. "Dishwasher is my preference. And I don't mean the soap suds and dish pan kind."

Sara stuck out her tongue. "For the few dishes I've got, it's dish pan and soap suds. Make your choice wash or dry."

"I'll dry if you'll help me put them away. Your kitchen and you know where things go." Drake walked up to Sara, held out his hand, and added, "Shall I escort you in, madame?"

"Certainly, sir. Leave the wine glasses. We can decide if we want to finish the wine with our smores." Sara laid her hand on Drake's. Heat sparked again and dissipated before her gaze met his. Drake shrugged and tilted his head toward the kitchen. She nodded. This chemistry of theirs was sputtering and sparking. Her gaze lingered on Drake's lips before she looked away. How much hotter and sizzling would a kiss be? Was Drake a sipper that kissed closed lips? Or a taster that enjoyed French kissing and tight full body hugs?

"Better watch where you're going." Drake laid his hand in the small of her back. Sara swallowed twice, wondering why her throat kept going dry. Warmth flowed out across her waist pooling just beneath the waistband of her leggings. The air around her got warmer. Chemistry again? It had to be the wine, right?

"I better. Makes things easier to clean up if they're not spilled everywhere." Sara moved away from Drake. Cooler air rushed over her. Proximity mattered? Flirting from across the room ignited some things like her imagination. This close up and touchable was new territory. One that required agility and adaptable learning.

"Care to share your thoughts?" Drake asked.

"May be later." Sara grinned and stopped near the sink. "I sorta fibbed earlier."

"Naughty. Naughty." Drake shook his finger at her. "How so?"

Sara laughed. "I do have a dishwasher other than these." She held up her hands. "Never enough dishes to run it other than holiday celebrations."

"Ooh, you got me good. I almost offered to wash." Drake pointed to the sink. "I'm fine with washing or drying tonight."

"There'll be enough with the crock from the crock pot, the other pots, and pans I used along with our dinner plates and utensils for the dishwasher."

"All right, I'll rinse. You load."

"You're on. We can both clear the table and put away the left overs." Sara set the chip bowl and pulled pork bowl on the counter.

Between the two of them, they had the table cleared and wiped down in ten minutes. Drake stood at the sink rinsing the crock out as she labeled the leftover containers. "We've got enough pulled pork for a couple more meals. Do you like salad?"

"Tossed salad is ok. I prefer a jazzed up mix." He set the crock on the counter.

Sara put the leftovers in the refrigerator. She opened the dishwasher and began loading it. "Jazzed up mix?"

"Tomatoes, croutons, olives, tangy dressing. Even meat. Warm meat adds a different texture to the mix." Drake handed her more dishes.

"Sounds interesting. I'm game to try it one night. I've got some packet dressing mixes we can make up along with things we can add." Sara placed the last of the dishes in the dishwasher and turned it on.

"More wine before I put it away?" She held up the bottle. It was still warm from the wine she'd poured back into the bottle.

"I've got enough left." Drake walked over to the table and picked up his glass. "Where are the smores makings?"

"Chocolate is in the cabinet over the dishwasher. Marshmallows are next to them. So are the graham crackers." Sara put the wine in the fridge.

"Where are the toasting forks?" Drake picked up the plate he'd put the chocolate, graham crackers, and marshmallows on.

"I've got them." Sara held up two two-prong meat forks with long metal handles. "I'll bring our wine glasses."

Drake set the plate on the coffee table. "The coals from the fire are red. Right temp to toast marshmallows. Do it now or later?"

Sara placed their wine glasses next to the plate. "We can toast a few now and more if we want them."

Drake pulled a chair from the table over close to the fireplace. He opened the fireplace door and turned toward Sara. "Ready for the first two marshmallows?"

Sara handed him a roasting fork with two marshmallows on it. "Go ahead with the toasting. I'm getting a chair."

"Okay. I've got an idea." Drake slowly turned the roast fork as he leaned forward. "Ever play twenty questions?"

"Yeah, why?" Sara sat down next to him.

"How about we ask each other ten questions a piece? Adds up to twenty. Different way to get to know each other." Drake leaned back, held out the fork to Sara. "Marshmallow for your thoughts."

Sara took a hold of the fork not too close to Drake's hand. She needed a break from sparks and chemistry to focus on the conversation. Her hormones could use the rest. So could her fertile imagination.

"How about this instead? We tell five things we would put on a profile on a dating site and why. It's a little more in depth." Sara laid a graham cracker on top of the chocolate, marshmallow and graham cracker she held.

Drake bit into his smore, savoring the sweet chocolate and marshmallow tang mixing with the crunch of the graham cracker. He wiped his mouth and said, "Sounds interesting. I'll go first. First item I would put on the site is been burned and not going there again."

"Oh my," Sara whispered. "What happened?"

Drake finished chewing and swallowed. "I—no make that we decided that we weren't good for each other."

"Weren't good for each other? How so?" Sara laid her smore on the napkin on her lap and reached for her wine.

"She wanted a fling, a short lived hot thing before she left. Never told me until the day before she left." Drake sipped his wine. "Me...I was falling for her."

Sara reached past her wine, took Drake's hand and firmly squeezed it. Heat seared across their palms. Drake grinned, holding her hand up. "Never had this with her. We're a hundred percent up on that level. Possibly more."

"What else would you put on your profile?" Sara let go of Drake's hand.

"Hmm, what would come next?" Drake sipped his wine, set his empty glass on the coffee table, and finished his smore. He turned in his chair until he faced Sara. "Next thing would be I want a relationship. No flings, no short term hot sheets and leave em. No wham bam thank you ma'am either."

Sara cleared her throat, glanced away, and asked, "You're wanting more than occasional hot sex?"

Drake took a hold of Sara's hand. "Thank you for attentively listening. You summed it up right. How does this make you feel?"

Sara looked up, her gaze not quite meeting Drake's. "Uhm...well..." She couldn't say more. How could she say intrigued without coming across as—as what? Turned on? Attracted? Definitely interested. That was the word. Interested. She wanted to know more. Drake intrigued her.

"I'm intrigued and interested. I'll share two things before you share another, okay?" Sara waited until Drake's gaze met hers as he spoke.

"Interested and intrigued are awesome. Gets me juicy in all the right places." Drake grinned. "If you need to know where I'm glad to let you know."

CHAPTER FIVE

Sara blinked, tried to grin and take a deeper breath. An image from her past flashed across her mind. A group of her five-year-old classmates talking about the difference between boys and girls. Thank goodness, the teacher had caught on before show and tell started. The image disappeared as Drake scooted his chair closer to her. "I'm waiting. What do you want on your dating profile?"

She pointed to her wine glass, and mimicked drinking. Drake nodded and handed her her glass. She sipped, pressed her lips together, took a couple breaths, and said, "I'm community oriented. I believe in giving back to the town I live in."

"Is that all?" Drake stood up, opened the fireplace door, and reached for the poker.

"No. It's a starting point. I believe in happily everafters. The kind where love abounds. . .but. . ." Sara didn't say more.

Drake stirred the coals, spreading out the remaining red coals to allow them to cool off. "Go on." He put the poker back on the rack and sat down.

"I got burned too." Sara faced Drake. "I'm cautious. Moving fast isn't me."

Drake nodded. "Another thing we've got in common. Burned, not quick to jump, and want more than a fling, right?"

"Sounds like it. What's your third and fourth items?"

Drake leaned forward, rested his hands, palms down on his knees. "I love my jobs. Firefighting and safety consulting. I trained at the fire academy in Chicago. I finished high in my class. Something about investigative work intrigued me. After a few years, I knew I wanted to make a difference."

'You'd put that on your profile? Why?" Sara yawned and stretched. "Excuse me."

"It's okay. It's been a long day for both of us." Drake stood. "Yes I'd put that on my profile. That is part of the reason I moved to Peyton Corners. Michael offered me the opportunity to interview for the Safety Inspector Job. Volunteering for the fire squad happened after the fact. Keeping people safe matters to me. I can do it from either job."

"Passionate about your work. That is an important thing to know. Too often people take a job because it pays the bills. I've had a few of those." Sara rose and picked up the plate holding the remaining graham crackers and chocolate. "The other two things I'd put on my profile are I love animals and starting over isn't easy. I moved to Peyton Corners because life in the big city isn't for everyone. Working in the hospital business office is fast paced, a challenge and allows me to put my graphic arts degree to work."

Drake followed her into the kitchen carrying their wine glasses. "We both moved to put our education to work. Take stimulating jobs we like. While starting a new chapter in our lives. We got a lot in common."

Sara put the wine glasses in the sink. "It seems like we do. " She yawned again. "Sorry. I'm usually in bed by now."

Drake put the chocolate in the plastic bag she handed him. "With the snow coming down hard, I doubt we'll be going much of anywhere tomorrow."

"I'm off weekends. You?" Sara added the graham crackers to the bag with the chocolate and put them away.

"Three day weekend. Unless I get called out. A full staff was on when I left the station." Drake leaned in, kissed her cheek, and stepped back. "Let's get your bed changed so you can crawl in."

"Thanks. McGee may try to crawl in with you." Sara moved to the edge of the kitchen doorway and stopped. "I can crate him."

"It's okay. I brought sleep shorts with me." Drake grinned and winked.

Sara laughed. "Okay. McGee snores some times."

"Can't be worse than an open bunk area full of men asleep on their backs. Our women crew mates have their own dorm room." Drake walked past her, pausing at the stairs. "I'd like to talk more about our chemistry tomorrow, please."

Sara waited until she was past Drake and part way up the stairs to respond. "That's a possibility. We'll have to wait and see. Patience is a virtue."

"It sure is. And your patience is going to be tried a bit. Our culprit is awake. I need to put the ash bucket outside after I clean out the ashes from our fire." Drake went back down the steps. "Come on McGee. One last potty run."

Sara smiled as McGee followed Drake into the kitchen. She'd count to five and see if McGee came running back into the living room. One-she moved up the stairs, paused on the landing. Two-Drake came back into the living room, waved and started clearing out the ashes. Sara went up the rest of the steps pausing at the top of the stairs. Three-McGee's barks sounded. Sara turned ready to stop the scamp before he made another wet mess in the middle of her bed.

Four-Drake called out, "Okay, McGee. You get another treat when you come back in."

Five-Drake glanced up as he held the ash bucket. "Go on, I gave him a biscuit to keep him busy. Now I'm opening the door."

McGee could be tricky. She wasn't going to stick around to find out. McGee and Drake could argue this one out on their own.

Drake set the ash bucket down near the back door. McGee eyed him, wagged his tail and backed up.

"Look dude, we have an understanding. You go water a tree quick and I put the ash bucket out at the edge of the patio." Drake opened the door. Wind whistle in and around the door. McGee backed up even more.

"It's damn cold out there. Let's be quick. You first. Me behind you. And we're back in before the wind can goose either of us, okay?"

McGee shook his head. Drake chuckled and opened the door wider. "On three McGee. We males can do it. One-Two-Three."

Drake leaned down, grabbed McGee's collar, and pulled him toward the door. He took a hold of the ash bucket handle in his other hand and stepped forward. McGee bulked, tried to prevent any forward movement. Didn't work.

Outside the wind buffeted them. Drake's curses were blown to oblivion. McGee stood close to the patio steps one leg barely cocked, head ducked, and piddle happening. Drake raced back to the steps. McGee already at the top of them. Another blast of wind rushed toward them. Drake stepped past McGee as they bolted into the kitchen and slammed the kitchen door shut. "Shit, that wind is vicious."

McGee ran up to the cabinet where his treats were, pawed the door and barked. He turned as Drake approached.

"Tell you what dude, you earned your treat. One more that's it." Drake opened the cabinet, quickly took one treat out of the gallon container Sara kept the treats in and tossed it to McGee.

McGee grabbed the treat and raced out of the kitchen. Drake shut the cabinet door making sure it latched before he exited the kitchen.

"Sara, inbound rascal with his treat," Drake called out as he reached the stairs. Except Sara wasn't there. He took the stairs two at a time, hoping she hadn't given up on him helping her make up her bed.

McGee bolted down the hall toward Sara's room. Little rascal could move. Short of the open door to Sara's room, McGee stopped. Drake halted a few steps back. Still, no sight of Sara. Drake glanced over his shoulder and back down the hall toward Sara's bathroom. Was she showering? Her bathroom door was partly closed.

McGee cocked his head from side to side. Wagged his tail and cocked his head again. Was he listening and watching for Sara? Drake moved up behind McGee glancing toward Sara's bedroom.

The bathroom door opened, slamming against the wall. Bang! McGee jumped, dropped his treat and bolted into Sara's room. Drake backed up against the wall, hands fisted, glaring at the bathroom door.

"What the?" Sara stood in the bathroom doorway, her arms full of sheets and pillowcases. "Spooked you?"

Drake let go a long sigh and nodded. "Caught me off guard. Very few have done that."

"Sorry about that. Linen closet is in the bathroom." Sara shifted the load in her arms. "Did I hear you say McGee was headed up stairs?"

"He was. I think he's under your bed now." Drake held out his hands. "I can take part of that. I'm supposed to be helping you."

"Thank you. First, we've got to get McGee out from under the bed. If he saw the crate, he's going to be way under there." Sara handed the sheets and pillowcases to Drake.

"Wouldn't it be easier to make up your bed first? Let McGee think he's one up on us. May be he'll come out on his own." Drake followed her into her bedroom.

"It might work. Especially if I put the dirty sheets in the laundry basket. He loves tipping the basket on its side and burrowing in amongst things." Sara stripped the pillowcases off the pillows and laid them on the trunk at the foot of her bed. "I hid the crate behind the trunk. Out of sight. Out of mind I hope."

Drake chuckled. "We'll know soon enough." He bunched up the top and bottom sheet, tossing them on top of the pillowcases. He held up the comforter. "Toss the comforter in the basket as a lure?"

"Not yet. Gotta get the sheets on." Sara billowed one sheet out over the top of the mattress. "Thanks for helping out. Getting the sheet tucked in all the way around takes a bit."

"Happy to help." Drake grabbed one corner of the flat sheet and tugged it toward him. "Why a flat sheet for the bottom?"

"Easier to make up the bed." Sara smoothed the sheet out on her side. "Toss em on the bed, tuck the ends and bed is made."

Drake copied her. "Makes sense. Easy and quick."

Sara snickered. "Easy and quick when you've got help. On your own it can take a few minutes to get everything tucked in."

Drake looked up and winked. "How about we meet in the middle and I'll tuck you in?"

Sara yawned. "I'll take a rain check. Maybe another night. We still have to get our chaperone out from under the bed."

Drake took the pillow Sara held out to him, tossing it on the bed. "McGee isn't doing a good job at chaperoning."

"Oh?" Sara laid the pillow she held on her side of the bed. She moved to the foot of the bed, lifting up the comforter. "Do tell why he's a bad chaperone?"

Drake came around the foot of the bed, stopped very close to Sara. "Because I get to do this." Drake slipped his arm around Sara's waist, hugging her tight to him as he turned to face her. "And this."

He slipped his other arm around Sara's waist and enveloped her in a full frontal body hug. "Mind if I give you a kiss good night?"

Sara let go of the comforter, leaned toward Drake, her lips puckered.

Smooth soft lips met his. Sara started to pull away. Drake moved back a step and held up a hand. "Thank you."

Sara smiled, leaned in, and brushed her lips over his again. "Thank you."

Drake looked away. The heat washing off Sara threatened to swamp him if he didn't get his horny id under control. "You're welcome. Now let's get McGee in bed so we can all get in bed."

Sara laughed. "Good pun!"

Drake wet a finger and drew a line in the air like he was adding points to a board.

Ten minutes later, McGee fussed about being in his crate after Drake almost crawled under the bed to get him.

As Drake closed his bedroom door, he couldn't stop smiling. Sara got to him. He got to her. They shared some things and had a few in common. Not a bad first date? Or was that not a bad part of a first date?

CHAPTER SIX

Friday Morning
Sara rolled over, squinted, and shielded her eyes. Daylight poured in through the slatted blinds covering the window across from her bed. Brightness yesterday afternoon and early evening didn't have. Either it stopped snowing or the sun was teasing her. A brief reprieve of warm brightness before the weather went back to overcast and more snow.

She grinned as she sat up. McGee slept curled up toward one end of the crate. He managed to fluff the towel she'd put with him into a heap that he'd burrowed partway under. Both of them had fallen asleep soon after she'd turned off the bedside lamp. Sleep hadn't evaded her like it had some nights recently. Maybe knowing Drake was around helped. McGee was good company. He couldn't play checkers or gin rummy. What was it her horoscope had said the other day? Her horoscope suggested human companionship. Well not quite that blatantly. It did talk about getting out and trying new things. Drake was new and the places her dreams had gone last night certainly were out of her comfort zone.

Sara stood, stretching as the clock on her bedside table came into view. *9:00 A.M.* McGee usually woke her up a few minutes before the alarm went off. She hadn't set the alarm. McGee was still asleep. She might get to shower without him fussing and barking.

A five-minute warm shower and back in the room before he woke up or started fussing. She grabbed her robe off the foot of the bed, slipped on her slippers and tiptoed toward the door. She hesitated as she reached the door. Not glancing back, she listened. No barks, no whines, and no scratching. Nothing ventured, nothing gained, and she wasn't waiting to find out if McGee was awake. Sara softly opened the door and stepped into the hallway.

Drake paused at the top of the stairs. He'd slept deep and sound in between dreams about he and Sara. Dreams he didn't know his conscience could come up with. Detailed, intimate and very sensual. He'd taken care of his urges twice during the night, grateful he still had laundry to do. Getting caught with jisim sticky underwear probably wouldn't forward his and Sara's budding connection.

He closed his eyes, focused his thoughts, and smiled. Creativity, imagination, and a set of hormones that clicked into high gear when Sara got near helped his dreams and libido rev their input. For now, images of a hot breakfast, coffee, and laundry took priority. Pork and scrambled egg burritos with hash browns. One of his special recipes. Michael referred to the recipe as simple easy hot bold. Hot bold if he added too much tabasco sauce. Sara's barbecue sauce had enough tang, the burritos wouldn't need any extra zip and zing added. Drake chuckled as he leaned down to pick up his laundry bag. As he took a hold of the bag, a yip and a bark sounded. He let go of the laundry bag. McGee was awake. Sara must be awake too. More barks and yips sounded accompanied by a low howl. Was Sara ok? Why was McGee carrying on?

"Hang on, McGee," Drake said, making his way down the hall. He stopped close to Sara's open bedroom door. She was in the shower. Maybe McGee needed to water his favorite tree.

Drake entered the room. McGee barked and whined as he scratched at the crate door. Drake opened the crate and stepped away. "Come on McGee. I'll let you out. Then give you a treat."

McGee rushed past him. Drake followed at a trot. In the hall, McGee paused, looked up and down the hall. Drake bypassed McGee heading down the hall toward the stairs. "Come on boy. The wind and snow aren't busy. So you can make your potty run quick and easy."

Drake glanced behind him as he reached the stairs. No McGee. Had the little culprit decided to squat elsewhere? Dang him. Clean-up was needed. Drake pulled a towel out of his laundry bag and started back down the hall.

"McGee! What are you doing? How did you get out of your crate?" Sara called out.

Drake skidded to a stop. Blinked, swallowed, and tried to divert his eyes. He couldn't. Sara stood in front of him—nude, holding a skimpy bath towel to her. McGee grabbed one corner of the towel, growling as he tugged the towel, pulling part of it off Sara. Drake lowered his gaze, not before he caught a glimpse of her areola and pink nipples.

"Sorry. I'll be downstairs." He slowly turned and flexed his hands. Part of him wanted to ask if Sara was all right. Part of him chastised him for lingering and not making a hasty retreat. No one ever said being courteous and sensitive was always easy. He called out as he moved down the hall. "Do you need help?"

"I'm fine. Thanks. I'll be down in a few," Sara replied.

Drake kept moving down the hall, only pausing long enough to grab his laundry bag and keep on moving down the stairs. He needed a distraction. A huge distraction. And it wasn't the hard on his psyche kept focusing on. Food, coffee—hot and sweet, and recipes. Cooking, breakfast prep, and . . .Did he apologize more? Or what? He caught his reflection in the kitchen window as he entered the kitchen. Was he blushing? Nah, must be flushed. He'd come down the stairs fast. Couldn't be that McGee caught both he and Sara by surprise! Could it? Mischievous little shit!

Sara let go of the towel, grabbed the edge of the bathroom door and shoved it partway closed. McGee jumped out from under the towel, tail wagging and barking.

"Shut up McGee!" She quickly put on her robe, tying it snuggly around her waist. Did Drake think she deliberately let McGee pull the towel off her? She bent down, picked up the towel and began to dry her hair. How did she apologize for getting caught off guard by a meddlesome four legged pain in the ass?

Sara grinned as she hung up the towel. She was at fault for part of what happened. Playing tug of war with McGee with his bath towel didn't help. McGee usually stayed in his crate while she showered. She put her slippers on and tossed her nightgown over her shoulder. One last look in the mirror and she . . .wait. . .Had Drake blushed? Actually embarrassed he saw her partial nude? Or did he use the word naked?

"Naked," she whispered, winking at her reflection. Shivering slightly as she repeated the word. Nude or naked. Both words meant sans clothes. Why did one carry a bit of naughtiness with its connotation?

McGee ran ahead of her, entering the bedroom. He went straight for the crate, sniffed it and started to lift his leg.

"McGee, you know better. Drake offered to let you out. Offered you a treat too. Behave or it's another bath and more crate time." Sara kicked off her slippers. She tossed her robe and nightgown on the bed.

McGee entered the crate and lay down. Sara nodded as she walked past the crate to her dresser. She pulled on her panties and bra, tossed a pair of socks on the bed. Moving to the closet next, she put on jeans and a sweatshirt. McGee let out a yip as she sat on the bed pulling on her socks and shoes.

"You can wait a couple more minutes. I'm putting my shoes on." She finished tying her shoes and stood up. "Come on McGee. Let's go get breakfast."

McGee bounded out the door and down the hall. Sara followed right behind him. Getting him outside was her main focus. As they reached the top of the stairs, delectable smells greeted her. Warm bread toasting, the tangy sweet smell of her barbecue sauce and a distinct sound. Was that Drake singing?

"Twice my heart threatened to bail

I know better now

Gotta listen to my heart

Hear the message it sends

Gotta know and understand

Falling for you

Yes I am, my dear

I got a feeling this time

My heart isn't going to bail"

Drake hummed as he placed the burritos in the oven. He turned, winked at Sara and walked over to her. He leaned in kissed her on the cheek and lips, pulled back and winked again.

"Breakfast will be ready in about ten minutes. Coffee is brewing. If McGee is ready, let's get him outside."

Sara gazed at him, her mouth moved, nothing came out. She nodded, turned around and exited the kitchen. Drake grinned, took the oven mitts off, and tossed them on the counter.

McGee ran into the kitchen wearing a bright red quilted dog jacket. He ran to the backdoor, barked, and wagged his tail. Drake looked outside, shook his head, and opened the door. Light snow fell, scattering in patches as the light breeze blew through the trees and down into the yard. McGee scooted past

Drake, sniffed the air and bolted out the door. As Drake closed the door, deep barks sounded. He glanced out the window. Where was McGee?

Drake looked out along the fence line, hoping McGee hadn't squeezed through the fence. One of McGee's barks sounded and a burst of red caught Drake's attention. Back and forth, up and down the fence line McGee ran one direction and turned around, bolting back the other. Another deep bark sounded and a large head appeared above the fence. McGee backed up, barking and making circles. He ran up to the fence, lifted his leg, whizzed and ran back toward the house. Part way back he squatted and left a pile.

Drake walked back to the oven checking on the burritos. "Nutso dog. Marking the fence is a new game."

"Boris is a friend. They're playing one up." Sara shook her head. "McGee thinks he's Boris's size and Boris thinks he's McGee's size. Cathy, Boris's owner and I laugh when the two of them get in the same yard. It's comical seeing a boxer crouching low and McGee running and jumping up like he's getting Boris's height."

Drake chuckled. "Like a cousin of mine's pony. He would prance and trot with his head and tail up when a draft horse came around. Shetland pony next to a draft horse. Sorta like McGee and Boris."

Sara grinned and nodded. "Yes. Quite a visual." She took a mug out of the cabinet and faced him. "Mind if I ask you something?"

"Sure. Go ahead." Drake took the mug from Sara and filled it with coffee. He set it on the counter and took the other mug she held out.

"The song you were singing earlier. Its sounds familiar. Did you write it?" Sara took the second mug from him, picked up the first and set them on the table. "Also, you 've got a nice voice."

"Thanks." Drake took the burritos out of the oven and set the pan on the counter near the plates he'd put out earlier. "It's by Blue Ridge Jazz. I know their piano player. Simon and I worked the same dining hall in college. He formed a trio with a college buddy of his, Karl and a friend's cousin, Anthony."

"Ever think of giving music a try?" Sara asked, taking a plate from him.

"For all of ten minutes. Singing in front of people just never felt right. I've done some back up for Blue Ridge Jazz on a couple of their songs. Firefighting and safety peak my interest. I like my job." Drake started to sit down at the table across from Sara as McGee began barking outside the door.

Sara pushed back from the table. Drake straightened. "I'll get McGee. You go on and eat."

Five minutes later McGee was curled up on the couch. Drake sat back down. "Let's eat before it gets cold."

Sara nodded. "I snuck a taste. These are good."

Several quiet moments passed as they ate, occasionally glancing at each other and smiling. Drake savored the last bite of his burrito, leaned back in his chair and sipped his coffee. If the last twenty-four hours were any indicator, he and Sara were off to a great start. What would the rest of the day bring?

CHAPTER SEVEN

Friday Mid-Morning

Drake dried the last plate stacking it on top of the other. He faced Sara. "I know you said you prefer to do the dishes by hand for only a few. With two of us here and cooking three meals a day, well. . .it's kinda."

Sara glanced at him, frowned and asked. "Kinda what? Slow? Soapy and wet?"

Drake sighed and shook his head. "Good come back. Not what I was getting at."

"Okay. Then what?" Sara hung the wet towel on the rack beneath the kitchen window. "I don't mind doing the dishes by hand. It's soothing."

"Soothing?" Drake leaned against the counter. "How so?"

"I sorta meditate. Get into the quiet. Listen to the birds outside if it's warm out. Or just enjoy nature's beauty. Even McGee and Boris running up and down the fence." Sara shrugged. "I shift gears then. Work is fully turned off and home is on."

Drake nodded. "Kinda like when I get a long weekend and head up to the mountains with my friend Parker. We camp and fish. Getting away out of town does that for me."

"If I get home early enough, sometimes McGee and I go for a walk." Sara exited the kitchen. "Do you like being outside?"

"Yeah. Camping and fishing are fun. Letting the fish go is the best part." Drake sat down on the couch. He patted the space next to him. "I've got an idea."

Sara sat close to him. "Idea?"

"Yeah, I need to go check on my place. It's a short walk there and back. Shouldn't take more than about ten to fifteen minutes to check on things.

Pipes, electric, and grab some more foodstuff from the freezer. I've got some nice steaks we can broil tonight."

Drake turned, facing Sara, watching and waiting for her response. The wind and snow had died down. The temperature—the sun in the sky and very few clouds—hadn't warmed up much above twenty-five degrees if he'd read the kitchen window thermometer right. Frack! It was colder than when he rushed over Thursday evening. Shit, what if his pipes had burst? Parker and Karl had said double insulating the pipes and solar panels were investments no homeowner should be without. Drake inhaled slowly. Whatever was going on at his place was what it was. That he couldn't change. Sara putting him off, he could do something about.

"Sara, if you'd rather not go. . ." Drake stopped speaking. Sara held up her hand.

"I didn't say I wouldn't go. I'm wondering if we should go now or wait to see if it warms up any more." Sara scooted forward to the edge of the couch. "McGee will think he's going for a walk if he sees me with my coat on. It's a habit. We'll have to sneak out on the kid."

Sara winked, pointed at McGee, and held a finger up to her lips. Drake moved closer and whispered. "Yeah, getting away from our chaperone ain't gonna be easy."

Sara grinned, motioning him closer. Drake closed the space between them until only a small space separated them. Sara blew him a kiss, and whispered, "Maybe we can behave 'cuz the chaperone isn't trying to liven things up."

Drake pressed his lips together. One snort, then another sounded. His shoulders started shaking. He pressed his lips tighter together. More mirth welled up threatening to blast forth. Drake started shaking his head and gave up. Laughter burst forth, Sara joining in. Their four-legged chaperone had his own agenda going and whatever it was, he was scoring better than the two of them talking and easing their way into things.

Sara knuckled away a tear, smiling as she did. "I haven't laughed that hard in a while. Thank you."

Drake entwined his fingers with hers. "Honey, you just moved up to the top of my list. I've dated very few women who get the absurdities of life. I love reading the comic strips B.C. and the Wizard of ID. They're good for a laugh."

"Oh I read those too. Irony and the moments where we can laugh at ourselves." Sara squeezed Drake's hand. "What list did I make the top of?"

Drake leaned in and kissed her cheek. "The women who intrigue me list. I'll let you in on a little secret about the list too."

Sara pulled back some, not letting go of Drake's hand. She rubbed her lips together, looked down at their joined hands, and back up at Drake. He watched her, almost intently as if he was afraid of her answer. Every time she touched Drake, heat flowed between them. He ignited a spark that she didn't want to go dim or go out. Drake was eye-candy, no doubt about it. She'd watched how other women had flirted, come on to him and oogled his shirtless pic in the community firehouse calendar. Mr. August was sitting next to her, holding her hand and...sharing secrets with her. He'd even kissed her. Did she want to know what his little secret was? Oh, yes she did.

Sara scooted back. She looked Drake straight in the eye. "You bet I want to know your secret."

Drake wet his lips, grinned and pointed at her. "You're number one on the list."

Sara blinked, stood up, walked away and came back. She sat back down. Pointed at herself, asking, "Me? How so?"

Drake leaned back on the couch. "You're going to find this hard to believe."

"I already am. Why haven't you said something before now?"

"You know the hours I work. Often double shifts. Late nights. Early mornings. Weekends. When do I have much time to date? How often have you run into me at Lindsay and Michael's?"

"Only a few times. I don't attend all their events." Sara stood again. "Let's talk while we walk. McGee upstairs."

McGee jumped off the couch and ran toward the kitchen. "Halt dude," Drake called. "That's not upstairs."

Sara laughed. "He thinks diversion will get him what he wants. Either a treat or more to eat."

"Boris did give him a work out." Drake rose. "I need about ten minutes to get my coat, gloves and hat. By the way, when we get back I need to do some laundry."

"Sure. Meet you back here in ten." Sara started toward the kitchen. "I got a chaperone to corral and crate. See you upstairs in a few."

"Come on McGee, let's get a treat. Then crate." Sara glanced back. McGee lay on the floor, his ears back, and his teeth showing. She shook her head. "Not gonna work, dude. If you want a treat, get your ass in gear or I'll carry you upstairs right now." She snapped her fingers and pointed at McGee. She turned and walked into the kitchen.

McGee ran to Drake. "Dude, I don't step between you and Sara. You best do what she says." Drake continued on to the stairs not looking back. He paused half up the stairs, partially turned, and softly laughed. McGee was running into the kitchen barking.

Drake reached the top step when McGee whizzed past him. Something hung out of his mouth.

"McGee, I said a treat. Not the rest of the box. Come back here," Sara called out.

Drake quickly moved to the doorway of his room. Sara was bounding up the steps, scowling and frowning. McGee was in deep trouble. Drake knew he wasn't going to get in the middle of that fight. Sara's tone and look said McGee had plucked her nerve good.

"McGee, drop it," Sara called out as she passed him. A bark followed by another sounded. "I said give me the box. You keep gobbling treats and you're going to be sick."

Drake started to turn around. Maybe Sara needed help.

"You can growl at me all you want. I've got the box. You're in your crate. I won and you get a time out." Sara exited the hall. She paused close to him. "Meet you at the door in ten minutes."

Drake nodded, catching the inside of his bottom lip with his teeth. What a sight? Sara's hair stood up in places. She carried a torn soggy box in one hand and what looked like a bunch of treats in her other. He didn't know whether to laugh, high five her or ask if the match was truly over.

He shook his head as he entered his room. He'd learned several things about Sara in the short time he'd been here. Three stood out. She had a sense of humor, could hold her own with their mischievous chaperone, and indicated she had an interest in him. *And there was their mutual chemistry.*

He quickly pulled on his hikers and socks, grabbed his sweatshirt off the bed and exited his room. Laundry could wait until they were back from their walk. As he started down the stairs one more thing he'd learned about Sara came to mind. She gave great conversation. Drake smiled more as his granddad's advice on women came to mind. Women could converse. If a woman gave great conversation, stimulating too, grab her up and show your interest. At that point, his granddad had leaned close and whispered, there's more to relationships and life than an awesome lovemaking. Not much, but a few things. Great conversation is one of them. Keeps you interested while you rest up.

Drake paused long enough to get his jacket and watch cap from the closet. He turned expecting to find Sara standing near the front door. She wasn't there. Was she in the kitchen by the back door?

"Sara," Drake called out. No response. Had she gone outside?

He zipped up his jacket as he made his way to the kitchen. Part way into the kitchen, he stopped, stuffed his watch cap into his jacket pocket, and gawked. Slowly, he moved forward. The scene in front of him wasn't what he expected or could have anticipated.

Sara sat staring out the patio door with her coat on. Several wadded up napkins lay on the table. The tattered treat box lay next to the napkins. Drake quietly picked up a chair, carried it around the table and placed it next to Sara. He sat down and took a hold of her hand. "Hi. I'm Drake. Mind if I join you?"

Sara glanced at him. "Nice to meet you, Drake. What brings you here?"

"You, my lovely lady. Been watching you from a far. Why so sad?"

"This." Sara picked up the tattered box. "McGee's fun. I like having you around too."

Drake grinned. "Glad I'm helping out."

Sara laughed. "I like where our first date is going. It works for us."

Drake rose. "Come on let's take a walk to my place. I've got a couple things I want to ask you."

CHAPTER EIGHT

Sara wrapped her scarf around her neck, zipped her parka closed and put on her crocheted hat. She patted her pockets. "Did McGee pull another pair of my gloves out of my jacket pocket?"

"You looking for these?" Drake held up a pair of gloves that matched her hat. "No McGee this time."

Sara ducked her head. "Yeah. He has a thing for my yarn basket. Loves to curl up in it if I have it out working on something."

"Are you one of the crafters that have stuff for sale at the fall craft bazaar?" Drake moved up beside her.

"Yes. Hats, scarves, and gloves. A few potholders and booties from time to time. How about you?" Sara exited the kitchen.

"Beyond posing for the yearly calendar, nothing else. Karl and Parker are talking about volunteering for the local scout troop. Chaperone a bunch on a campout." Drake opened the front door.

"You offered to chaperone?" Sara stepped out onto the front porch.

"I like kids. Chaperoning a group of them, not sure how well I'd do. Want kids someday. They say you learn from taking care of others. Parker says he'll let me gain experience with his and Angela's twins." Drake pulled the door shut behind him as he stepped out onto the porch next to her.

Sara laughed. "Door is locked. Experience comes in many different ways. What about your niece?"

"I'm the youngest child. My siblings had married and moved out by the time I was thirteen." Drake stepped off the porch and moved on down the walk. "My parents died in a car accident. By the time I found out about my niece and a couple of nephews, I was in college on my own."

There was something about Drake's response. Cold and quick? Or did his fast reply indicate there was more than what Drake said? The small amount of information Lindsay had shared about Drake made a bit more sense. He offered to work most holidays. Signed up for extra shifts so his co-workers could have time off for family events. Family-oriented and yet a loner? Sara nodded. She could relate.

"Hey Drake," she called, following him. "I'm sorry if I said something wrong."

Drake halted. Sara's question had hit a nerve. One that he usually handled better. Seeing her sitting in the kitchen with tear-stained cheeks, gut grabbed him more than he cared to admit. He distracted himself when the loneliness got to be too much, threatening to overwhelm him. He enjoyed hanging out with his pals. Even spending a few holidays with Karl and his fiancée Tanya and her two boys. Parker and Angela often included him when either of their families were in town. Sometimes though, he felt like the odd person out. No one to actually connect with or bring to festivities. Christ, the moments he and Sara had spent in the last few hours filled him with ...

What? You know you're feeling connected? So why not admit it? You're falling for her, right? He wished his damn conscience would shut up.

You clam up and miss a chance at something good. Unique and worth pursuing. Take a breath. Open up a bit more. Chemistry is great. Connection is even better. Trust is important. Trust your heart to tell you what's right.

Drake rolled his shoulders, flexed his hands and did an about-face. Thank goodness, his conscience hadn't shut up. Last time he'd connected and fallen for someone quickly, it had horribly backfired. Sent him running from himself and trusting only a few people. He could continue to let the past hold him hostage and keep him trapped in the expectation any other relationship he tried would turn out the same. Or he could let go and take a risk on reaching out beyond the obvious. Small steps led to bigger ones. He was making one more.

"Sara," Drake began, holding out his hand. "Thank you for the apology. You didn't say anything wrong."

Sara took hold of his hand. "Okay."

He squeezed Sara's hand and let go. "Some days my past reaches out and sucker punches me. I like what we've got going on. How about you?"

Drake glanced away. Man, his palms were sweating. He shoved his hands into his jacket pockets. One breath in. Exhale slowly. Another breath in, deeper this time. He slowly exhaled again. He'd stepped outside his comfort zone. Put himself at risk with his question. Would Sara's answer sting? Hurt? Or . . .

Bring you joy. Ignite a spark that bonds with the other sparks already percolating between you. Listen with an open heart. You'll be okay.

Nobody ever said listening to their conscience and heart was easy.

Do you think it's easy watching you get hurt? No. We share in the joys, pain, and other things that go on. We aren't always logical. We watch, listen, and try to make sense.

Drake looked up. Sara's gaze met his. She was smiling. He took a breath and smiled.

"Drake," Sara said, moving closer to him. "I like what we got going on too. We're getting to know each other in a way most people don't. I think that's good."

"Me too. It's risky. Yet. . ." What was the word he was looking for?

"We're friends and one odd part is we're neighbors too. It's not like a blind date." Sara leaned in and kissed his cheek.

Drake laid his hand on Sara's arm, tilted his head, and brushed his lips over hers. Sparks, red bursts of color and bright blues flashed behind his closed eyes. The steady beat of his heart told him he wasn't afraid. He'd taken the chance and found a bit of joy. Sara liked what was happening between them so far. Maybe he could let his guard down some more.

"Yup, no blind date. It's a bit unnerving that Saturday night we do have a sort of official date." Drake swiped his hand against the inside of his jacket pocket.

"We got partnered up for the community social. We don't have to call it a date. We could even call it a second date. That way there's no first date expectations. We're getting them out of the way." Sara smiled. "I'm looking forward to walking in with you."

Drake snickered and shook his head. "Make 'em wonder. Ooh, I like your devious mind."

Sara chuckled. "Not devious. Let them think what they want. We know what's going on. I definitely like what we got going on."

Drake walked a bit down the sidewalk, stopped, and held out his hand. "Shall we practice how we're going to walk in Saturday night?"

Sara grabbed his hand and squeezed it. "You bet. We can practice kissing too after we get back from checking on your place."

Drake opened his mouth and quickly closed it. Sara had just scored several points pushing her rank higher on his interest list. She'd caught him off-guard.

"Ah-h. Ok-k." He glanced at Sara. She nodded, winked, and pointed forward.

"Let's go see how your place is. I know you're worried. You can stay with me as long as you need to." Sara moved forward.

Drake shrugged and followed her. Another point for Sara. She wasn't afraid to lead or voice her opinion. He'd watched his parents bicker over who was in charge, who spent what, and other small crap until they hardly spoke to each other. Their 'I love you' lacked warmth, sincerity and any feeling unless he made his presence known. They faked it in front of him very good. He rolled his shoulders. He had choices. He made one. Sara.

Moving up beside Sara, he raised their joined hands and held up his other hand. "Put your other hand against mine, please."

Sara faced him, raised her hand, and pressed her palm tight against his. Drake rubbed his left cheek against his bare hand and Sara's gloved one. He did the same with his right cheek. Spurts of warmth nudged his cheek and palm. Nothing like what happened last night. No pulsating heated throb pounding its way into his heart, groin and conscience. Had their connection cooled?

"Take your gloves off and cup your hands together in front of me." Drake slid his hands away from Sara's. Sara quizzically looked at him, at her hands, and back at him. She smiled as she took off her gloves and stashed them in her coat pocket.

"Is this what you mean?" Sara held her hands up, flexed her fingers and put her hands together like she was ready to pray.

"Yes," Drake whispered, closing the space between them until they stood only a short space apart. Raising his hands slowly, he inhaled. Bursts of pink, yellow and blue caught his attention as the clouds parted and the sun illuminated both of them. Sara's hat colors framed her like an aura glowing with joy, caring and . . . What was it Karl's sister-in-law had said when she did his tarot card reading? *Yellow is the path to your heart. You are looking for the one who lights your inner candle. You will know when her golden glow pierces your heart and ignites the fire of your inner love.*

Sparks, heat, searing warmth met his palms as he cupped his hands around Sara's. He waited until her gaze met his. He opened his mouth and slowly exhaled. Slowly, ever so slowly, as if time almost stood still, he exhaled, blowing the heat from deep in his heart outward. He closed his mouth as the last air blew out. Inhaling deeply, he held his breath as he counted. He wet his lips and spoke, verbalizing what he'd drawn from his heart moments before. "Sara, I'm falling for you."

Sara leaned forward until her forehead rested on Drake's. Her gaze not leaving Drake's. She puckered her lips and brushed them over their hands. She licked the tips of two of Drake's fingers, suckled them into her mouth, and flicked her tongue rapidly over them. She let them go and whispered, "I'm falling for you, too. You're important to me."

The wind wasn't blowing. Drake's cheeks were red due to something else. She'd watched many guys' looks rove over her or some of her women friends. Drake's was tantalizing her. Memorizing each part of her as if he committed her to memory. He blew on their hands one more time and lowered his hands. She lowered hers.

"Let's go check on my place. I need the distraction." Drake turned and walked away from her.

Sara grinned. He hadn't turned too quickly. Probably with a good reason too. The front of his jeans was tented. She'd gotten to him. His hot and steamy gaze had caused her nipples to tighten. Maybe more than kissing was going to happen when they got back to her place.

Drake glanced over his shoulder. Sara watched him. Heat welled up inside him. He couldn't have hidden his hard-on if he wanted to. She'd given him the hot once over he'd never expected to get from anyone. Sex was great. Orgasms were delicious with the right partner, but connection, chemistry and part of his heart were in this too. Maybe, he hoped he was right; this hotter, higher connection included her heart too.

He turned, held out his hand. Sara closed the distance between them, clasping his hand as she got even with him. Warmth skirted across his palm, wrapping its tendrils around his wrist as if a higher power bonded them together. Whatever was happening, Drake knew he was listening to his heart and inner voice more.

CHAPTER NINE

As he and Sara approached the gate of his front yard, Drake noted his feelings, his heartbeat and gut. Other people he'd brought home were people he trusted implicitly. People he knew and understood. Their character and ethics stood out. The last woman he'd taken through that gate was two thousand miles away. She'd broken up with him the same night he brought her to see his new home. The night he'd planned on popping the question. Here he was with someone different, someone he'd gotten to know and yet still had much to learn about.

He took hold of the gate and let go of Sara's hand. "Welcome to my place. I hope what we find inside doesn't scare either of us."

Sara laid her hand on his arm. "Don't sweat it. I'm here because I want to be. I'm here as your friend and neighbor. Right now, it's about what you and your home need. Whatever we find, we'll get through it together."

Part of him screamed don't trust anything Sara said. Trust came with vulnerability. So did living. He ducked his head, checking with his heart, gut, and conscience happened now. No flip-flopping going on gut-wise, check. His heart beat calmly and strongly, check. Conscience—was it snoring?

Hey dude, gotta grab rest when I can, you know.

Drake softly snorted and raised his head. He pushed the gate open. "Thanks, Sara. I appreciate that a lot. Let's go on in."

Sara entered, pausing by the front steps. "The outside of the houses all look the same until you stop to look at them. You chose the stained glass window for your front door. And the twisted wrought iron railing for your bannister."

"Actually, the designer did. He offered me a huge discount if I took what he had left. I like stained glass artwork. The tree of life design reminds me of my trip to Ireland and Scotland. The wrought iron allows air to flow through and the breeze reaches through the screen when I have the door open."

"Practical and artistic. Do you have pictures from your trip?" Sara followed him up the steps.

"Packed away. There are boxes all over the place. I've not had much time to settle in. You'd think three months would be enough time." Drake unlocked the front door. "After you. Welcome to my place."

Sara wiped her feet on the burlap doormat and took hold of the door jam. In a moment, she would enter Drake's space. She'd been in the house on her tour of the homes left in this section of the complex after a new builder and contractor bought the original builder out. Half-finished rooms, unpainted walls, and incomplete plumbing and electrical work. The contractor and builder had explained what she could have as basic parts of finishing out the unit. She'd often dreamt of what this unit would look like finished and the model as the original builder had planned. Now she was about to find out. She stepped up and entered.

A deep russet brown and burgundy afghan tossed on the catty-cornered couch across the living room grabbed her attention. She knew that stitch and pattern. The afghan had taken two months to complete. Extra-long and wide to cover a bed had been her intent. To see the familiar piece here in Drake's place—did he know she made it? Her labels said made with tender loving care and her initials. Nothing more. How could he know?

"Something wrong?" Drake moved around her. "You okay?"

"Yes," Sara whispered. She cleared her throat and repeated, "Yes, I'm fine. Caught off guard by that." She pointed at the afghan. "I often wondered who bought it."

"You made it?" Drake entered the living room. "The colors spoke to me. Earth tones appeal to me. The few years my parents and I lived in the southwest were golden years. Peace, love and joy-filled our family."

Sara laid her hand on Drake's arm. "I can relate. I love gardening. Being outdoors. Of course, when it isn't so damn cold and snowy."

Drake laughed and patted her hand. "True. Climate is what we got. Weather is what we expect. And every once in a while it's a coin toss."

Sara grinned. "For sure. Where do we need to check first?"

"Do you mind checking the kitchen and half bath? I left the faucets open. I want to get any useable foodstuff over to your place."

"Boxes or bags to put it in?" Sara started toward the kitchen.

"Empty boxes are fine. There shouldn't be much. I'll do a quick check upstairs. Be back in about ten minutes." Drake scampered up the steps.

Sara entered the kitchen. Even though the original layout mirrored hers, Drake had changed it up. On the back wall, a large side-by-side combination refrigerator and freezer occupied most of the space. Where her sink and window overlooking the backyard were, Drake had put sliding patio doors. She could make out the covered grill that set to one side of the doors. As she approached the doors, she gasped. He put in a hot tub? The small cubical tub sat across from the grill. At the farthest end of the patio, a three-section screen partition blocked the view from the other yards bordering his.

"Ingenious. Privacy. And luxury. I like." Sara turned, spotting a medium-sized box near the patio doors. She noted the small stream of water running out of the sink faucet. The open door must be the half bath. She quickly crossed the room, taking in Drake's decorating tastes. Mid-tone wood cabinets lined the area above and below the sink. She opened the one closest to the sink. Her grin grew. A concealed dishwasher, two-thirds full of dishes. There were a few pots and pans in there. Drake did some cooking. A thud sounded, drawing her out of her thoughts. She quickly closed the dishwasher. Sounds of running water greeted her as she flicked the light on in the half bath. Behind the door, the stackable compact washer and dryer took up most of the floor space of the half bath.

'Efficient use of space." She picked up the box, set it on the counter and opened the refrigerator. She checked good through dates before setting items on the counter to pack in the box. In the freezer, she found typical guy food, a frozen pizza, a bag of mixed vegetables, a half-empty box of hamburgers and an unopened bag of French fries. Another thud sounded as she picked up the box and exited the kitchen. What was Drake doing upstairs?

Drake tossed another shoe into his closet. Three pairs of work boots and two sets of running shoes lay scattered across the floor when he first entered the room. Shit, he needed to straighten up.

Dude, it's too damn cold in here to worry about that. Check the damn bathroom and get back downstairs. A warm house and steamy passionate kisses await you at Sara's.

Drake caught his wily grin in his dresser mirror as he crossed his bedroom. Images of him and Sara cuddling on her couch making out flashed through his mind. Yeah, warmth on two levels was better than the chill causing his breath to fog when he exhaled. He made a fast check of the bathroom. Water trickled out of the sink and shower faucets. He ran back into his bedroom, grabbed a duffle bag out of the closet and stuffed a few more items in it along with a pair of work boots. As he reached the top of the stairs, he glanced toward the kitchen. Sara exited, carrying a box that appeared full of things.

He slung the duffle bag over his shoulder and reached for the box as he reached the bottom of the stairs. "I can take that."

Sara shook her head. "It's not heavy. Eggs, milk, a partial loaf of bread, a frozen pizza, and a half box of burgers. Stuff we can use at my place. Unless you want that bag of mixed Chinese vegetables too."

"That was from a batch of stir fry I made last month. Tried to use them up but they don't do well in a pot of soup." Drake opened the front door. "Come on, it's cold in here. I hope the weather breaks soon so the electric comes back on."

Sara exited first. He locked the door and followed her. One thing he knew for sure, he wanted to follow through with getting to know Sara better and be her date for Saturday night's dance.

He waited until they were on the sidewalk before he asked his question. "Sara, there's something I need to ask you."

Sara turned, balancing the box on her hip. "Sure. What is it?"

Drake leaned close, kissed Sara's cheek and opened his mouth to speak. Instead, a loud gurgle sounded, followed by a belch. He quickly closed his mouth, took two breaths and tried to speak again. "Sorry."

"No harm. No foul." Sara grinned. "I think the one thing you want to ask about is food."

"Yeah, and show me how your washer works?" Drake held out his hand. Sara took it.

"Food and clean clothes. Two of the ways to get a man's attention." Sara raised their joined hands and kissed them. As she lowered them, she added, "There might be a few other things I want to show you too."

Sara took off down the sidewalk before he could respond. "Touché," he muttered. "Touché." She'd scored several points, piqued his interest and more. Now if his cock and balls would stop sending smoke signals to his libido and horny id, he might get some laundry done and part of a pizza eaten. He was going to need all the strength he could muster if that twinkle in Sara's eye meant what he thought it did.

Halfway back to her place, Sara set the box down, gathered up a handful of snow and faced him. "Oh, Drake." She grinned and motioned him to come closer with her other hand.

Drake shook his head, stopped and dropped his duffle bag on the ground. "What's your plan with that?"

"What?" Sara patted the snow between both hands. "This?" She held up one hand, displaying a lopsided snowball.

"Yeah, that." Drake scooped two handfuls of snow and started patting them together. "No ice balls. See I only got snow."

"You saw me get only snow. I call who gets snow-covered most cooks the pizza." Sara trotted toward him, her hand back, ready to fling her snowball.

Drake ducked behind the sapling at the edge of his yard. Poof! Snow littered the air. Sara had hit the tree. He stepped out from behind the tree and tossed his snowball. Whizzed right past Sara who was bent over grabbing more snow. Damn, her jeans outlined her pert ass real nice—whiteout! Double damn, her second snowball hit the tree and with the wind's help, scattered snow on him.

"I scored!" Sara called out, running back toward the box.

Drake ran to his duffle bag, grabbed the two handles, balancing his snowball in one hand, and took off after Sara. Halfway back to her place, he flung the snowball at her. It landed on her boot. "Yes! I scored!"

Sara raced up her steps and set the box down. "Tied score. Guess we both have to cook the pizza."

Drake moved up beside Sara. "I'll help you spice the pizza up before it goes in the oven. With the leftover pulled pork and some of the spices I brought over, we'll turn that plain cheese pizza into a rival of Mama Lucia's."

"Sounds delicious." Sara unlocked the door, turned around and grinned. "Here's your surprise for being a good sport on our snowball fight."

CHAPTER TEN

F*riday Afternoon*
    Sara cupped Drake's face, pressed her lips to his and parted them. Drake didn't hesitate. His tongue met hers. Her hands slid to Drake's shoulders, pressing herself tighter to him. A full deep passionate French kiss on the front porch!

She pulled back, rubbing her lips together. Drake's toothpaste mixed with hints of his sweetened black coffee. He tasted divine. He hadn't run from the kiss. He gave as good as he got. "*WOW!*" she whispered.

"Double wow!" Drake backed up. "Glad your neighbors aren't watching."

Sara laughed. "You never know." She picked up the box.

Drake glanced over his shoulder, turned bowed and turned back.

Sara pressed her lips tight against each other. Two steps into the house...and she clapped her hand over her mouth. She set the box on the living room end table closest to her, dropped into the chair next to it, and clasped her sides. Peals of laughter rang out.

"Well, got to let them know the show is over. " Drake set his duffle bag on the staircase. He closed the door, stuffed his hat in his jacket pocket, and hung his jacket on one of the coat pegs near the front door.

Sara sat up and took off her jacket. Drake held out his hand. "I'll hang it up. You need help getting up?"

"Thanks. I'm fine." Sara rose. "I'll take the box into the kitchen. If you're going upstairs, would you mind letting McGee out of his crate? I'm sure he's fussing."

"Sure. I'll let him out." Drake leaned down and kissed her cheek. "Meet you in the kitchen in a few."

Sara picked up the box and walked into the kitchen. She put the perishables in the refrigerator and left the pizza on the counter. Mama Lucia's was Peyton

Corner's top pizzeria and Italian restaurant. Drake had a recipe that rivaled Mama Lucia's? Sara licked her lips, remembering the last time she ordered from Mama Lucia's. X-large with pineapple, ham, mushrooms and cilantro. She'd had leftovers for lunch and dinner for a week.

"Sara," Drake called out.

Sara went to the living room. "Yeah."

"Watch out, McGee inbound. Or is that outbound?"

A flash of red, followed by a yip and the scampering of paws down the stairs sounded. Sara snapped her fingers. "Come McGee. Outside."

McGee ran past her, twirled around in a circle, barking and pawing at the back door. Sara opened the door and McGee shot out into the yard.

McGee leapt off the porch and made a beeline for the tree almost middle of the yard. It was like the scamp got bashful about pottying in view except when it came to Boris. Sara shook her head and walked back to the counter. She put the pizza in the fridge, glanced out the window; McGee was still sniffing and watering the tree.

"Drake," she called out as she got to the edge of the kitchen."

"Right here," Drake said, coming down the stairs.

"Any crate cleanup needed?"

"Taken care of. Shredded pad and a few wet spots on the floor from leakage." Drake glanced at his watch. "1:15 already?"

'Thanks for helping with clean up." Sara started back into the kitchen. "Hard to believe it's that late already."

"McGee ready to come in?" Drake glanced out the kitchen window.

"Probably. He's hiding behind the tree doing his duty." Sara opened the door. "Watch out the whirlwind is about to enter."

Drake nodded and crouched. Grabbing McGee before he made a beeline for the stairs wasn't going to be easy. "I'll corral 'em and get his coat off."

"Bedroom doors?" Sara asked, opening the door more.

"Closed. Bathrooms too. We might outfox 'em this time." Drake cupped his hands between his legs. "Come on home McGee."

Sara snickered. Her last two short-lived tries at a relationship had ended abruptly. She ended them. No one screamed and yelled at McGee. Much less cussed him out. He was her fur child and deserved understanding. Drake and

McGee seemed to be getting along. Drake even helped without being asked. He scored huge points for that.

McGee raced toward Drake. Drake leaned forward. McGee veered to the right. Drake leaned to the right. McGee switched directions. Drake copied McGee's moves. McGee yipped and picked up speed, heading straight for the small opening between Drake's legs.

If she were betting, she'd take even odds on who was going to win. It might be a toss-up. McGee appeared to be in the lead.

"Oh no, you don't." Drake dropped to his knees and rolled on his side. McGee halted, backed up and barked. He put his head down, growled and rushed toward Drake again. As he reached Drake, McGee jumped up.

"You need more spring and bounce to get over this hurdle." Drake sat up, firmly holding a squirming McGee between his hands. "Settle down. Let me get your coat off and you *might* get a treat."

"New box, second cabinet over from the door. After what he did to the last box, I don't trust him." Sara took the leftover burrito ingredients out of the fridge.

"Dude, how do you get so muddy? It's like you're jumping in the mud every time you go out." Drake let McGee go. Holding McGee's muddy wet coat out in front of him, Drake stood up. "This needs washing."

"Toss it in the basket of towels on top of the washer. I'll put them in while our pizza cooks." Sara set a pizza pan on top of the stove.

"Help you with the pizza in a moment." Drake walked past her, grinning.

Sara gripped the edge of the sink. She got McGee from the local animal rescue. He'd rescued her as much as she rescued him. McGee loved her unconditionally. She loved him too. But, she missed human companionship.

Were she and Drake rescuing each other? Not in a 'save me' way. Instead, they were chancing being vulnerable, letting their scared, hurt leery sides out and finding healing from that. Healing in a very special way. Drake and she connected. Quietly understood each other and yet had much more to learn about each other. Knowing Drake was here filled her with . . .with curiosity, concern, and desire. Something she hadn't felt in some time. Lindsay had mentioned Drake was younger than Michael by about a year. Sara let go of the sink as the laundry room door opened. How would Drake handle her age?

Drake walked up to her, leaned in and brushed his lips across her cheek. "Thanks for getting the pizza makings out of the fridge."

Sara pulled a chair out from the table and sat down. "You're welcome. I want to talk about something before we make the pizza."

"Okay," Drake sat in the chair opposite her. "What's up?"

Sara licked her lips, laid her hands palms down on the table, and said, "I'm a year older than you. How do you feel about that?"

Drake covered her hand with his. "I turned thirty last year. I've dated women younger than me, my age and older than me. Some were very mature for their age. As one older woman put it, experience adds to the person. She out bowled me every time we met for our weekly bowling match and at seventy-five, she was a firecracker."

"You're okay with the age difference?" Sara asked as Drake's gaze met hers again.

"Sure am. I see you. I don't see a number. I gathered from our talks and what Lindsay and Michael have said about you that you lived fully. Firefighting and rescue work aren't for the faint of heart." Drake rose, walked over to the fridge and took out the cheese pizza. "Don't worry. I want someone I connect with. Shares similar values and understands friendship is an important part of a relationship. You gotta like and respect each other first. Love is built on that."

Sara pushed back from the table. She walked over to Drake, slid her arm around his waist, and hugged him. "Thanks. Let's get the pizza made. I'm hungry."

Drake had used the L word. Was he hinting at he was falling in love with her already? Damn, her jittery stomach. Could she let go of her suspiciousness and ask the big question? *You love me already?* The last guy who said it only wanted sex. That had blown up faster than a lit match fizzled out.

"Ok. My clothes basket is in the front room. Probably with a muddy McGee fast asleep in them. Let me get them and we can work on the pizza while a load is washing." Drake exited the kitchen without waiting for Sara's reply. Her tone and stilted hugs spoke loudly something bothered her. He could let it pass or talk about it. Asking questions might uncover something. From their discussions, they'd moved beyond 'hi nice to meet you' hadn't they? Damn, assuming could make an ass out of both of them if either of them kept on supposing.

He chuckled as he reached the couch. McGee was sprawled on the couch on his stomach with all four legs out to the side. Drake hesitated as he reached for the basket. Was McGee snoring? Yes, McGee was. "Enjoy your nap McGee." Drake picked up the basket and reentered the kitchen.

"Any trouble getting McGee out of the basket?" Sara asked, opening the laundry room door.

"He's sacked out on the couch. Wasn't in the basket." Drake followed Sara into the laundry room. "Nice, you have side by side washer and dryer."

"Instead of a half bath, I chose the utility room option." Sara pointed to the shelf above the washer. "Laundry detergent and dryer sheets are there. If you need pretreat, it's in the cabinet along with the non-chlorine bleach."

Drake set the basket on the dryer. "Settings look pretty self-explanatory. Let me get this load started."

Sara exited the laundry room. Drake glanced over his shoulder. She hadn't flinched when he brushed past her entering. Nor had she put distance between them like he'd offended her. He added detergent to the load, closed the lid and pushed the start button.

He had the two questions he wanted to ask in mind as he exited the laundry room. Sara stood at the stove with her back to him.

"Sara, did you put the oven to preheat?" Drake set the container of leftover barbecue meat and shredded cheese on the table.

"Yes. I oiled the pizza pan too." Sara held up the bag of cilantro. "How much of this do we need?"

"A couple handfuls. Tear 'em up in small batches to add to the pizza on top of the barbecue and cheese. I usually do a layer of each. Then pop the pizza in the oven." Drake spread cheese and barbecue on the pizza. "I have a question."

Sara looked up. "Uhm, okay. What?"

"What did I say earlier that upset you?" Drake slid the pizza across the table to Sara.

She picked up some cilantro and sprinkled it on the pizza. "Remember when you said letting go of the past isn't always easy?"

"Yes, one of our first talks after I moved in. We laughed over finding things in mislabeled boxes." Drake picked up the pizza and put it in the oven. He set the timer and came back to the table. "Does this have to do with something from your past?"

CHAPTER ELEVEN

How did she respond? Parts of her past colored her reaction. Sara knew some people easily used the L word and like interchangeably as if the two words meant the same thing. She'd seen and heard a few folks use the L word to get what they wanted, sex or a fling. She'd almost fallen for it three years ago. Hearing people say the word had freaked her out for several months. How did she explain this? How did she be that vulnerable and stay open to hearing what he had to say?

Her palms were sweaty. Her heartbeat was steady. Checking in with herself like her counselor said and listening to her heart put her in charge. Sara closed her eyes and listened for her inner voice, her heart.

You focus on the here and now. Clarify what Drake means and discuss your needs. You matter.

"Let me preface what I'm about to say with, this isn't about you directly, ok?" Sara rose, went to the sink and took a glass out of the cabinet. She filled it half full of water and sat back down. "Four years ago, I was in a six-year-plus relationship. Part of the time, we were long-distance. Zach traveled for work and was in a part-time residency grad school program. In between work travel, he'd travel to Arizona to do his two-week residency for the program he was in. Boy, did all that turn out to be a bunch of crap."

Sara sipped her water. Drake didn't say anything. He nodded and motioned for her to continue.

"Zach had several friends with benefits relationships going on. He never told me about them. His grad school residency was a cover for the time he spent with his fiancée. He used the word love as an endearment and supposed expression of how he felt about us." Sara drank the rest of her water. "Two years ago, a guy who I was dating off and on kept saying he loved this and that about me. When I confronted him about it, he said, isn't that what women want to hear. I don't fear the word. I want to know that the person saying the word isn't just using it loosely or trying to use it to get me to have sex with them."

Drake placed his hands palms down on the table. He leaned forward as he spoke. "I'd beat the shit out of Zach for not being honest with you or any of his sex partners. Much less his fiancée. As to the dude using it to get into your pants, he needs his mouth washed out with some nasty tasting soap and needs quite a few lessons on treating people with dignity and respect."

Sara flashed him a weak smile. "Thanks. You do get this isn't about you."

"I do. I also get you're uneasy because I said something about love. I want you, desire you, and am feeling very connected to you. I'm not ready to use the L word to describe us. We don't fit the normal pattern of a first date or blind date given we're neighbors, friends and sorta roomies." Drake flipped his hand over, palm up. "How about we take this at our pace? Stop means stop. No means no. And we check in with each other. I want you to feel safe, heard, cherished and respected."

"So you're saying. . ." Sara stopped speaking.

"I take that is an open-ended question."

Sara nodded.

"All right, we go the speed we're both comfortable with. If you need to stop, we do. If you want to go forward and I am ready for that, we do. Each of us is in charge, sound good?' Drake started to turn his hand over. Sara slid hers under his. Heat scalded across his palm searing its jagged way up his wrist as it wrapped itself around his arm as if to brand him with its intensity.

"Drake," Sara began. "I think our connection heated up more."

"I agree." Drake leaned forward, his mouth open, ready to say more.

BEEP! BEEP!

Drake took his hand off Sara's. Cool air rushed over his wrist and forearm. He pushed back from the table. "I don't know if we were saved by the timer or the timer saved our lunch."

"Probably both. We do get focused at times." Sara stood. "I'll get the plates and pizza cutter. Do you want wine or root beer?"

Drake chuckled as he set the steaming pizza on the counter. "A bit early for wine. An ice-cold frothy root beer sounds good. We could make root beer floats with the ice cream I brought over last night."

"After lunch, sure. What about with the pizza?" Sara set the plates next to the pizza.

"Sparkling water with lime?" Drake opened the fridge. "Quenches your thirst, a bit of sweet tang and goes nicely with the pizza."

"Better than soda. Naturally sweet and fizzy enough to tingle your taste buds." Sara placed two glasses on the table. "Sparkling water it is."

Drake walked back to the table with two bottles. "Pizza cutter?"

"Silverware drawer next to the sink." Sara sat down. "Hope that pizza tastes as good as it smells."

Drake set a plate in front of her with a slice on it. He slid his plate across the table to where his glass and sparkling water bottle were. "Don't wait for me. Dig in. We can talk when we're done eating."

Sara bit into her slice. Heat trickled across the front of her tongue, growing in intensity as she chewed. Sweet spicy barbecue tang mixed with the cilantro's nutty intensity warmed her mouth and taste buds. She swallowed as Drake sat down. "Unique combination. The heat and hint of Latin spiciness followed with American sweet and Louisiana spices. How did you figure out Mama Lucia's recipe?"

Drake chuckled. "I didn't. I came up with my own. Being assigned cooking detail for twenty hungry fire fighters is not easy. I gave Mama Lucia my recipe."

"You gave Mama Lucia your recipe?" Sara took another bite of her pizza slice.

"More like the crew bragged about my pizza when Mama Lucia asked them why they'd stopped ordering as often. She offered to swap recipes with me. I agreed real quick." Drake took a bite of pizza, chewed and swallowed. "Mama Lucia gifted me with a basic cookbook and five of her basic recipes: homemade meatballs, chili spaghetti, chicken parmesan and a basic alfredo sauce."

"Maybe you should be doing the cooking." Sara grinned as she opened her bottle of sparkling water and filled her glass. "Sounds like you got the know-how."

"I got to keep the basic recipes. Michael ruled the cookbook belonged to the station. That way whoever had cooking duty could come up with a decent meal." Drake wiped his mouth. "Now you know something not many people know. I can cook."

Sara held up her glass. "Here's to good meals, good times and more."

Drake touched his glass to Sara's. "To good food and good times. I hope the more includes you and me."

Neither said more as they lowered their glasses. Their gazes met as they ate in companionable silence. Questions, concerns and ponderings flooded Drake's mind. He remained silent. Asking Sara what she meant by more might come across as pushy. Would she explain or was he going to have to ask?

Sara finished the last of her slice, wiped her hands with her napkin and pushed back from the table. She waited until Drake looked up to speak. "We've discussed a lot. Learned more about each other. Yet there's a something we haven't said much about."

"I'm listening." Drake laid the crust from his slice on his plate.

Sara swallowed the last of the sparkling water in her glass and set it down. "We're attracted to each other. Admitted our desire, but are we ready to go there?"

Drake grabbed his napkin and covered his mouth. If he lowered his napkin, he'd spit water everywhere. Caught off-guard by a direct question. Sara earned a huge amount of points with that. He swallowed his mouth full of water. "You're racking up points. Caught me off guard again."

"You're keeping score?" Sara pushed back from the table.

"Hold on. It's not a tit for tat kind of thing." Drake laid both hands palms up on the table between them. "Darlin' you rate. You're awesome. I like that you catch me off guard. You speak your mind. You're authentically you. You're my top choice for who I want to spend more time with and get to know better."

"Thank you. We're doing well in some main areas like communication and attraction." Sara toyed with her water glass, turning it back and forth. Did she ask the question that kept coming to mind or ignore the butterflies fluttering in her stomach? She drank the rest of her water, set the glass down and pointed at herself and Drake as she asked, "Are we playing it safe because we're fearful?"

"What if we are? Is that so bad?" Drake put the plates and glasses in the sink. He leaned against the sink as he continued speaking. "Are we ready to step outside our comfort zones together? Take a large change at trusting each other more?"

Sara stood. "Is it really a change? We trust each other or we wouldn't be here."

Drake rinsed his hands, shook the water off them, and tore a paper towel off the role next to the sink. He patted each hand dry and tossed the paper towel on the table. He kept moving forward until he stood toe-to-toe with Sara. He reached up, cupped her face, lips puckered. Would she kiss him or turn away? He was ready to trust her with his heart. Was she ready to trust him with hers?

CHAPTER TWELVE

Sara looped her arms around Drake's neck, brushed her lips across his, snuggled closer and whispered, "What about birth control?"

Drake leaned back. He stared at her for several moments, opened his mouth and quickly closed it.

Had she caught him off guard again? His mind wasn't on sex or intimacy? Or was he taken back by her upfront question? Taking care of herself also took care of him. An unplanned pregnancy wasn't fun for either parent. She wasn't ending up like two of her cousins; oops pregnant, married, and divorced all within a year. She doubted Drake was irresponsible. She slowly inhaled, focusing on Drake and her inner energy.

"Sorry to catch you off guard again." Sara slowly slid her hands off Drake's shoulders and onto his upper arms.

Drake shook his head. "No, not off guard. I had similar thoughts. Wasn't sure when to bring it up."

Sara rubbed her hands up and down Drake's arms. "We're getting closer and closer to acting upon something. Chemistry, attraction, and our growing connection. Perhaps the big question is, are we interested in taking things further right now?"

"You—you mean here and now?" Drake stepped back from her a couple of steps.

"Not in the kitchen. Not on the table either." Sara moved back and to the side. She held her hand out to Drake, "I think we need to continue discussing this."

"Where?" Drake loosely entwined his fingers with hers.

"The living room. Sitting on the couch?" Sara squeezed Drake's hand. "I seriously want to talk about this."

"Sure." Drake let go of her hand, closed the space between them, and kissed her cheek. "I think both of us are ready to move outside our comfort zones together."

"I agree. Sometimes the biggest obstacle is getting around ourselves." Sara exited the kitchen. "I like you. I enjoy our friendship. Our connection is strong. We've got something going."

"Yes, we do." Drake sat down on the couch. "Do we want to talk about what we want out of this first?"

"After we discuss safe sex and birth control, sure. If we change topic, we've let intimidation win again." Sara sat down next to him.

"Intimidation?" Drake rested his palms on his knees. "I'm sorry I scared you like that."

"You didn't. What's cropped up is past experiences. We've each had them. Been dumped. Forgotten or misinformed." Sara propped her feet up on the coffee table.

"Good summation. And spot on." Drake swiped his hands across his jeans. "The one that stands out for me is misunderstood."

Sara nodded. "Yeah, that too. Back to the main topic, safe sex and birth control."

Drake rose and walked partway to the front door. He turned. Sara's gaze met his. "I'll go first, okay?"

"Sure."

"First, I get tested quarterly. Required for my EMT continued certification. Two, my last results were clean. Nothing communicable. Three, I believe birth control is both partners' responsibility." He paced the length between the coffee table and door again. As he turned, Sara patted the couch.

"No need to pace. I'm not out to get you. This is about both of us. I'm ready for my turn." Sara drew her legs up on the couch.

Drake sat down. "I'm open to questions."

"Thank you and I've got them. I'll ask them in a few." Sara hugged her knees to her. "I'm used to being tested from when I was a medical receptionist. I do it monthly since I volunteer at the family planning clinic twice a month."

"Good to know. I like you give back to the community. Go on."

"I'm clean. No disease or communicable diseases. I agree with you a hundred percent that both partners are responsible for birth control." Sara let go of her legs and turned toward him. "What questions do you have?"

"Preferred birth control?"

"Condoms and the pill. Backs each other up. Nothing is foolproof."

Drake grinned. "Oh, yeah. My granny used to say if you don't want kids, don't let go of the aspirin you're holding between your knees."

Sara snorted. "That's good. I like that. I might use that in the sex education class I teach at the community center."

"Go ahead. It makes sense. I have one more question."

"Okay."

"Are you on the pill?" He leaned back against the back of the couch.

"Yes. Just started a new pack. My menses is over. Do you have condoms with you?" Sara scooted closer to him.

"To say no would be a lie. The one in my wallet is possibly over a year old. Do you have some?" Drake held his hand out. "If not, there's another trip to my place happening."

Sara stood, holding out her hand. "I have them. I believe in being prepared."

"You're ready to use them now?"

"I'm a lover. Not grab you and do it type." Sara walked over to the stereo. "Tomorrow night is the dance. I don't know what kind of music you like besides Blue Ridge Jazz. Do you prefer fast dances or the slow couple close-up dances?"

"Both. There are some fast ones that are close-up couple ones. Country line dancing is fun. I've taken a few classes down at the recreation center. What's your preference?" Drake stood.

Sara flipped through the CD tower next to the stereo. "My fave band is Crescendo Heart. They play a mix of soft rock, folk, and a bit of jazz. They're a local band."

Sara inserted the Cd she pulled out from the tower. A soft lilting melody began, followed by the chords of a string guitar. The singer spoke of a love born in the moment. Passion igniting as two strangers found each other. Two hearts beating in almost perfect unison. Sara turned around, holding her arms out. "Dance with me?"

Drake closed the space between Sara and him. He slipped one arm around her waist, taking her free hand in his. "I'd love to dance with you."

Back and forth they swayed, letting the percussion move them. Drake stepped back, drawing Sara with him. She easily followed his lead. "You're a good dancer."

"Thank you," Sara tossed her head back. "High school gym teachers felt my graduating class needed to learn etiquette which included couple dancing."

"Sounds like the advice my senior class advisors gave us. I remember it well." Drake cleared his throat and spoke in a deeper toned voice. "Boys and girls, there is more to dancing than standing in one place shaking your behind like it's on fire."

Sara snickered. "Got a similar talk. A few of us enjoyed the classes. Some met the person they took to prom. Those that tolerated it made sure there was plenty of fast dances too."

"Need to keep folks moving and grooving as my dad used to say. Music gets your feet and body going." Drake moved them in a circle around the small space between the couch and entertainment center. "I like how you feel in my arms. I hope there's a bunch of slow dances Saturday night."

"Me too." Sara nestled closer, resting her head on his chest. "Let's keep dancing a bit more."

Drake cuddled Sara tighter to him and kept moving them in side-to-side steps around the space through two more songs. As the third song ended, Sara pulled back. Her gaze met his. "I want you."

He nodded, glancing toward the couch noting McGee slept on. "Corral McGee first?"

Sara grinned. "Yes, our chaperone isn't doing such a great job, is he?"

Drake chuckled. "Well, maybe the music got to him too."

Sara leaned in, brushed her lips over his, and let go of his hand. "I'll let him out for his last potty run while you get the bribe ready."

"Oh, I get to be the bad dude. Thanks!" Drake started toward the kitchen.

Sara scooped McGee up off the couch, carrying him into the kitchen as she followed Drake. Their chemistry continued. As did the ease with which they worked together. There was more than desire or lust going on. Was she falling for him?

"We're both bad dudes. He hates going outside after dark with no coat." Sara opened the door, put McGee down, and nudged him out the door. He looked up at her sleepily. "Out you go. You got five minutes."

As McGee started to turn around, Sara closed the door. "Oh, he'll be pissed when he comes back in. He'll go for the biscuit if you let him back in."

Drake grabbed two biscuits out of the box, put the box back in the cabinet, and trotted over to the door. "Poor McGee. He's gonna make a beeline for your bed with cold, wet feet."

Sara hugged Drake to her as she moved up beside him. "Why do you think I am getting a head start on getting him into his crate?" She slid her hand down over Drake's stomach, past his belt, stopping just above his pubic hairline. "See you upstairs."

Drake glanced over his shoulder at the door as Sara patted his ass twice. Corralling McGee was going to be sweet and simple, right? Images of him and Sara undressing each other flashed across his mind. He curled his hand tighter around the biscuits. "McGee," Drake called out, moving closer to the door. "I hope you got your engine revved ready to fly up the stairs."

CHAPTER THIRTEEN

Drake opened the back door. Mid bark, McGee raced in the backdoor, around Drake and picked up speed as he exited the kitchen. Drake opened his mouth, closed and reopened it. McGee was flying low and super revved up.

Drake flicked off the light as he exited the kitchen, calling out. "Sara, McGee incoming. Hope you are ready."

As he reached the steps, Drake sighted Sara running down the hall with McGee hot on her heels. No easy catch of their chaperone tonight.

"Come on, McGee," Drake called out. "I got treats. Two of them."

No bark. No yip. He raced up the steps, two at a time. "Sara," he called out. Silence. Great, had she cornered McGee in the bathroom with the door closed or had he run into the closet like he had tried to earlier?

Drake slowed as he entered the hallway. The main bathroom door was open. Sara's bedroom door was open. Had McGee darted under the bed again? Drake crept up to the door and looked in. McGee sat atop the crate, wagging his tail. Sara sat on the bed, her hand over her mouth.

"You can tell me later how he got up there. Let's get him inside." Drake held out his hand, palm up as he approached McGee.

Sara nodded. She lowered her hand. "Try distracting him with one of the biscuits. I'll grab his collar. That will keep him from escaping."

Drake nodded, holding one of the biscuits out. "Hey McGee. Got a treat for you. You ready for it?"

McGee glanced at him, back at Sara, and back to the hand coming closer holding out the biscuit. Drake moved his hand up and down. McGee's head bobbed up and down following the motion. "Good boy. I got another one here for you." Drake waved both hands up and down.

Drake leaned closer, holding one biscuit out more than the other. McGee rose, yipped, and lunged for the biscuit. Drake dropped the other biscuit, stepped forward and—Sara's hand curled around his. He looked down. Both their hands were wrapped around McGee's collar. "We got 'em."

"That was too easy. " Sara slipped her arm under McGee's stomach and scooped him up. "Stop squirming. You're going to bed. Drake and I are going to bed." Sara glanced at him and winked. Drake swallowed hard.

"Toss the other biscuit inside. It'll distract him." Sara leaned down, holding McGee with both hands. McGee squirmed more.

Drake tossed the second biscuit in the crate. "I'll get the door."

Sara leaned down aiming McGee toward the opening. "Here's to him not getting by us."

Ten minutes later, McGee barked twice, grabbed the second biscuit and burrowed under the bundle of blankets in the opposite end of the crate.

Sara looped her arms around Drake's neck. "Chaperone corralled. Now where were we?"

"About to get the box of condoms out of the bathroom and adjourn to my room. Away from prying chaperone eyes." Drake stepped away. "Lots of hot water, soap, and towels await us. First how did McGee get up on top of the crate?"

Sara snorted. "He came running up the stairs, leaped up trying to nip me. I ran down the hall with him chasing me. I ducked behind the bedroom door. He didn't slow down as he entered the bedroom. He spun around trying to find me, leapt up in the air as he spun and bumped into the crate. Watching him trying to scramble to keep from landing on the floor was hysterical. I couldn't stop laughing."

"Flying dachshunds. A new species we'll have to see if we can capture them on film." Drake chortled, slipped his arm around Sara, and kissed her cheek.

"Indeed. We have other experiments awaiting us." Sara snuggled closer to him, whispering, "There's enough room in the guest bath, two of us can shower at the same time."

"Can't say we have naughty thoughts happening. Plenty of soap and water await us." Drake pointed forward. "Shall we see how wet and soapy we can get?"

Sara laughed. "Oh, yes. We aren't likely to run out of hot water either. Not that we plan to take a long shower."

"Nope. Wet, soap and rinse. Some nice slippery wet caresses and cuddles mixed with some steamy kissing. What you think?" Drake paused outside Sara's bathroom.

Sara fanned herself. "Got me steaming already. Hope the heat doesn't overwhelm us too quickly."

Drake laughed, stepping into the bathroom door. "That is why there's a fan in there to dissipate the heat and steam. See we're prepared. Where are the condoms?"

Sara hesitated at her bathroom door. Kissing, hugging and touching with clothes on was different than being nude and vulnerable. There was nothing to hide behind once their clothes came off. Would the chemistry change? Lessen or . . .She clenched and unclenched her hands, shook them, and chafed her arms. Fear, the one large rock in her stomach, grew with each breath she took. Flashes from the past rose in large waves, racking her psyche until she shook. Two guys had walked away because she wasn't a size 8 or could wear a bikini. Not that she wanted to. Skimpy clothing that barely covered anything wasn't worth the worry about what if it fell off. Drake had seen her in shorts and tank tops, even a one-piece bathing suit. He knew she didn't have a model's figure. Still getting undressed took away that last layer of cover and protection. Was she ready to go there?

"Hey, what's wrong?" Drake cupped her chin. "Having second thoughts?"

Sara raised her gaze until she looked Drake straight in the eye. "Not second thoughts. Fear thoughts. Past experience welling up and blasting away my confidence."

"Uncertainty is a kicker. What can I do to help?" Drake lowered his hand and moved closer. He reached for her hand. "If it helps, feel my heartbeat. It's fast, slow, then fast. I've got the what-ifs. The lovely game my past loves to knock me upside the head with. What if this happens again or this."

Sara nodded. "We're going to take off our clothes and what if the chemistry fizzles out?"

"I think we're beyond that already. You saw me in my underwear. I saw you partially nude. We're still kissing, hugging and flirting. I'd say chemistry is still happening." Drake looped his arm around her neck. "What do you think?"

Sara grinned. "Thanks for illuminating the positive."

"You're welcome. I put my doubt to rest with our talk. How about you?"

Sara stepped back and moved around Drake. She opened the medicine chest door. She picked up the box of condoms, read the expiration date, exhaling slowly. She turned, holding out the box. "I like we can talk things out. I'm more at ease too. How about we each take a piece of clothing off and check-in before we go further?"

"Sounds intriguing. Let's us move at a pace that's comfortable for both of us." Drake took the box from her. "Where would you like to undress? Bedroom or bathroom?"

"Bedroom. Your bedroom." Sara edged away from the bathroom doorway. "One less set of eyes if you know what I mean."

Drake laughed. "Oh, yeah. My mom's cat was named Voyager after some Sci-Fi TV program she watched. I called the damn cat voyeur. "

Sara pressed her lips together. Images of a younger Drake trying to undress with a cat watching him popped up. What was it with animals and their need to gawk? She waved her hand. "I can so relate. McGee does that too. That's why I keep a blanket over most of the mesh part of his crate. Trying to dress with someone watching your every move gets a bit unnerving."

Drake entered his bedroom. He set the condoms on the nightstand. "Voyeur had a thing for socks. She'd grab them and run through the house with them. The stinkier, the better. Even the vet couldn't figure out why she did this. We knew to look under the couch for the missing mates. "

"McGee used to shred paper. Leave a piece lying around and he would shred it. He did it for a while with his toys too. He spent a lot of time crated as a puppy." Sara leaned against the door jam.

Drake sat down on the bed and patted the space next to him. "Sit down and be comfortable."

Sara gripped the door jam with both hands. One step forward—and she was saying yes. Saying she was ready to take a chance, a risk and be vulnerable in a different way beyond neighbors and friends. Was she ready to make that leap of faith?

She let go of the door jam and took a step forward. "Why does now feel so different? We kissed earlier. Hugged and touched."

Drake smiled and nodded. "There's intent. Declared expectations. My palms are sweaty. My stomach has the flutters. It's like facing a fire."

Sara sat down on the edge of the bed close to Drake. "Like facing a fire?"

"Yes, no two are alike. You use the knowledge you have, know experience doesn't mean this fire is like any other. There may be similarities, but nothing is exactly the same." Drake leaned toward her as he continued speaking. "Being aware, focused and in conscious connection with yourself and what's going on all around you helps." Drake touched his chest close to his heart. "I know here I care for you a lot. Focusing on that keeps me mindful about both of us. What is your heart telling you? Do you trust your heart?"

Sara inhaled slowly. The flame inside her flickered each time Drake touched her, came close, and—having him around ignited heat and desire she hadn't expected to feel after the last jackass called her a cold limp fish with no passion. Kissing that idiot was like sucking on a mouth full of ice. He took without giving. Demanded and expected her to keep on giving no matter how she felt without regard to her needs. Two words came to mind...hollow and shallow. Was she measuring Drake by those same words?

"Trust is a mixed word. I trust me in many ways. I've gotten burned trusting others too much. Healing your heart isn't easy. Especially when someone you thought loved you, even said the words, looks you in the eye and laughs as they tell you they lied." Sara covered Drake's hand with hers.

"Why do people think they can play with a person's heart? Even attempt to tear their soul apart?" Drake scooted closer to her. "I've had a few friends like that, male and female. Even a relationship I fell hard for. She was looking for a fling. Use, get what she could and dropped me like a piece of discarded trash. I was ready to propose."

Sara faced Drake. "We're both leery, burned and leery. Are we ready to trust ourselves and each other? Listen to our heart voice deep within and take a risk on there being more."

CHAPTER FOURTEEN

"Actions speak louder than words." Drake bunched the hem of his t-shirt in both hands. "Let me show you." He worked the shirt up and over his head, off his arms, and dropped it on the bed. He took Sara's hand and laid it on his bare chest, close to his heart. "Want and desire can mix with lust. The heat flickers and poof it goes out when lust is sated."

Sara tried to pull her hand away. He laid his hand on Sara's arm. "Please don't pull away. I want you, desire you, and know I need more than just physical release."

"What do you mean?" Sara laid her other hand on his chest close to her hand.

"I care for you. You and McGee are part of my world. Part of what I look forward to when I come home. Your smile. His crazy antics. Even our talks across the fence. I wouldn't be here if I didn't." Drake lowered his hands. "I'm a lover. Not a user."

Sara nodded, sliding her hands slowly down Drake's chest. Firm, warm and inviting. He leaned into her touch until her palms and his abs were tight together. She looked up, Drake watched her. No scowl, no frown. A soft smile and a gaze that lingered on her face, not taking inventory like she was a piece of meat. Slowly, very slowly, she leaned in and brushed her lips across Drake's chest. "Soft and warm. I like what I see and feel."

She drew her hands back, reached under her top, and undid the clasp of her bra. She worked each strap down and over each arm. The same with the other. Drake sat still, watching her. Somewhere deep in her psyche, worry disappeared in a puff of smoke. Her stomach stopped trying to meet up with her heart. Calm and desire mixed together in a way she hadn't felt for quite a while.

"Here's the piece I'm taking off." She tossed her bra on the bed close to Drake's t-shirt. "How we doing?"

Drake brushed his knuckles across her cheek. He leaned in and pressed his lips against hers briefly. "I'm good. You?"

Sara exhaled slowly. Drake's response eased over her inching its ways deep into her core, her heart and psyche. The confident, soft tone turned her on because he was keeping his word. His actions and words were backing each other up. She wet her lips. "I'm doing good, too. I could use a hug."

Drake held his arms out. "When you're ready, I'm ready."

Sara scooted closer until their legs touched. She put her arm around Drake and leaned against him. Drake laid one arm loosely along her shoulders and his other across her stomach.

Sara tilted her head back. "Thanks for taking things slow and talking them out. I'm ready to take another piece or two of clothing off."

Drake nodded. "You set the pace. You've got a few more things on than me."

Sara smiled. "We both have socks on. How about jeans and socks?"

"Okay, but then I am down to my briefs. You still have your panties and top." Drake started to lower his arms.

"Jeans and socks in here. Rest of our clothes in the bathroom? Kinda evens things out."

"Let's do it." Drake stood, unzipped his jeans and shoved them down his legs. He hopped on one foot as he pulled his sock off and worked his pant leg over his foot. "One more to go. Or you want to do one of yours first?"

Sara stood, toed her socks off, bent over and picked them up. She held her hand out, clutching her socks as she straightened up. "Socks off. You want to sit down and try getting your last one off without falling down?"

"Gee, thanks for the advice. Not that I am falling down." Drake started to push up off the bed from where he leaned against the bed trying to keep his balance.

"No, you aren't. I think I'll go next instead just to be safe." Sara unzipped her jeans. "I guess you're too busy trying to stand up to watch so I'll. . ."

Drake shoved himself upright, turned around and flopped down on the bed. He turned on his side facing her. "I'll watch from here. This view is better."

Sara pushed her jeans down barely past the waistband of her panties. She turned around, bent over and worked her jeans partway down her hips. She straightened and faced Drake. "Enjoying the view?"

Drake held up his hand, splayed his fingers and dragged them down through the air twice. "You're scoring ten plus ten, honey. Delicious view."

Sara blew a kiss at Drake and winked. "Well, time has come. . ." She stopped speaking, rushed to the bed, stopping close to Drake. "to undress you!"

She yanked Drake's remaining sock off, grabbed the leg of his jeans and backed away pulling them with her.

Drake tried to sit up. His sweat-covered palms slipped along the quilt offering him no chance to halt his increasing slide toward the edge of the bed. "Come on. Wait I don't need—-" Him, his jeans, and his descending briefs were heading toward the floor if Sara kept pulling.

"Oh, you don't? How about we both need to—" Sara let go of his jeans, turned and stripped hers off. "Meet you in the bathroom."

Sara trotted out of the room. Her paisley pastel-colored panties appeared sliding down her hips. Was she losing them or. . .Drake sat up, cussing, he shoved his jeans and briefs down and over his feet, kicking them aside as he strode toward the bedroom door. He bet Sara wasn't losing her panties. The minx was probably taking them off.

Sara stood by the bathroom door. Entering signaled she was ready to let Drake see her nude. He'd briefly seen her nude thanks to McGee's tug of war antics with her bath towel. Now she was making the decision. Taking the chance and risking—risking what? Rejection? Drake not liking what he saw? If that were happening, he wouldn't be standing behind her.

"You okay?" Drake asked, coming up behind her.

"Yes." She faced Drake. Once again, he was outside his bathroom, only this time he was nude. Sara grasped the hem of her shirt, pulled it up and over her head, and off both arms. She tossed the shirt aside. "Kinda evens things up."

Drake held out his hand. "I'm ready for a shower."

Sara pushed her panties down her hips and legs. She kicked them aside as she stepped out of them. She took Drake's hand. "Me too."

Drake's gaze roved over her. His eyes met hers. "I like the view." He stepped back. "Your turn?"

Sara nodded, taking her turn. "I like," she said, her gaze meeting Drake's.

Holding hands, they entered the bathroom. Drake faced her as they reached the shower. "Warm, soapy and quick?"

"Yes, please." Sara took two towels off the shelves over the toilet and laid them on the sink counter.

Drake slid back the shower curtain, stepped into the tub and held his hand out. "Come join me. We'll save water, up the temperature, and . . ."

Sara took his hand. "Oh, the temperature rose quite a bit out there in the hall. We haven't even begun to see how hot we can make it."

Drake pulled the shower curtain closed. Not much space separated them. Heat rose between them and he hadn't even turned the shower on yet. Sara reached past him, her arm brushing against him. He didn't need to look down to know how she affected him. His desire was evident. Sara held her hand up, a bar of soap filled it. "You turn the water on, please. I'll wash your back if you'll wash mine."

"Water coming. There's more than your back I'd like to wash." Drake brushed his lips over Sara's, turned around and glanced down. His cock erect, hard and ready greeted him. His attraction to Sara hadn't cooled.

He turned the faucet on halfway between hot and cold. Warm water rushed out, splashing over his feet. Drake glanced behind him. Sara held the soap. Would he last long enough to let her soap and rinse him? He hoped so.

Drake turned sideways. "Water warm enough?"

Sara moved forward, her hand and hip brushing against him. Her hand grazed his cock. She glanced at him, smiled and stuck her hand under the water. "Both are warm and inviting."

Sara faced him, cupped her hand around his cock and balls, and slipped her other arm around his waist. She closed the space between them until her breasts touched his chest. Drake put an arm around Sara's waist, pressing tighter to her. "Uhmmm. .." He couldn't say more. Words failed him. Heat, deliciously intoxicating heat roared off Sara, searing deep into him.

Sara pressed her lips on his and pulled back slightly. "Soap is wet. We're partially wet. Time to soap and rinse? Or we can continue enjoying our mutual touching." Sara tightened her cupped hand around him.

"I love your touch." Drake brushed his lips over Sara's. "Touching you is more than a wow. It's mind-blowing." He stepped back.

His palm up, he slid his hand under Sara's breast, lifting it slightly. "To be with you here like this is awesome." He leaned down, lips puckered, and suckled her nipple. He stopped as Sara started squirming. "Knowing that I turn you on and you want to be here with me like this set a spark off deep within my heart."

Sara laid her hands on his shoulders. "I want you. Not for a quickie or to walk away the morning after. I sense your passion, your desire and your genuine caring."

Drake held his hand out. "May I wash you?"

Sara laid the soap in Drake's hand. She moved past him, ducked under the shower spray and faced Drake. "Yes, please wash me," she murmured, moving out from under the shower.

"Sure. Arms up." Drake stuck his hand under the shower. "Lots of suds or just a bit?"

"Some suds. You wash, I rinse. Then I wash you. You can rinse while I dry off." Sara raised her arms.

"Sound like a plan. Soap-suds coming." Drake worked the soap between his hands. "Ticklish?"

"I think I'll let you find out." Sara started to turn around.

"No. Front first." Drake reached toward her with a soapy hand.

She nodded, facing Drake. He grinned as he laid the soap in the soap dish. He rubbed his hands together, soaping both of them. He closed the small space between them, raising his hands as he did. He intertwined his fingers with hers. Squeezed her hands briefly and start a slow soapy slide down her arms until he reached her shoulders.

CHAPTER FIFTEEN

Drake waited until Sara's gaze met his. Anticipation could be very intoxicating. He trailed the tips of his fingers down and over Sara's taunt sensitive nipples and partly back up over them. Around and over her areola, coming closer to her nipples with each circle of his fingers.

"Hmm," Sara murmured. "That's good. Are your nipples as sensitive?"

Drake leaned in, brushed his lips over Sara's, and replied, "You'll find out on your turn."

"Need more soap?" Sara asked, holding the bar of soap out.

"Might." Drake swept his hands lower, laying his palms flat against Sara's ribs. Circles clockwise, then counterclockwise until he reached the edge of her pubic hair. He looked up. Sara watched him. His hand glided lower, down over the soft hair of her pubis caressing his palm until his finger slipped between the lips of her mons. One stroke. Then another. Over across and around her clit until ...

Sara vibrated each time he stroked her clit. Small murmurs, rapid sighs. Her nipples grew tauter until. .

"Yes," Sara moaned. "Goodness yes." She tossed her head back, tightening her hold on him. "Oh my, it's so good."

Drake slowed his strokes, stilled his hand and fingers. He slowly slid his palms up across Sara's stomach until he reached her waist. "Soap, please." He held out one hand. Sara laid the bar in his hand and turned sideways. Drake wet and lathered his hands and laid the bar of soap back in the dish. "I'll get your back."

Sara turned around, facing the shower. She wet her hands, lathered them and quickly washed and rinsed her face. "Drake," she began looking over her shoulder. "How about I wash you next?"

Drake's soapy hands rubbed up and down her back for several moments without him responding. She started to turn, wondering if she said something wrong. As she turned more, her worries dissipated. Drake faced her. His desire stood out, pointing at her. She reached down and loosely folded her hand around his cock.

"Easy," Drake groaned. "I'm real close to ejaculating."

"I turn you on that much?" Sara flexed her hand, squeezing Drake slightly.

"Did, are and still am." Drake jerked toward her as she slowly squeezed and released as she worked her hand up and down his cock. On her last squeeze, Drake took hold of her arm.

"Sweetie, I love you touching me. I'm so hard. So turned on much more I'm going to squirt all over your hand." Drake started to drop his hand.

Sara brushed her lips over Drake's. "Quick soaping and rinsing. I'll let you take care of your cock and balls. I'll get the rest. Sound good?"

"Marvelous." Drake held up the bar of soap. "Soap away."

Sara thrust her hand into the spray of the shower, rubbed the bar between her hands and laid the soap in the dish. She stretched her arms out, soap-lathered palms down, as she laid them on Drake's shoulders. "Arms out, please."

Drake held his arms out, his palms toward her. Sara glanced to each side and back at Drake. "No tickling either."

"I'd give you a raised hand promise, but I'm a bit busy at the moment." Drake winked and blew her a kiss.

Sara laughed. "Yeah, me too." She swept her hands down off Drake's shoulder, over his pecs and stopped. Muscle and warmth. . .She could feel Drake's heartbeat. Steady strong beat. His body and heart were sending a message that her heart heard. Her psyche absorbed and delighted in. Drake spoke the truth. Fear went up in a puff of grey smoke as if it surrendered and knew its time to cease had come.

She brushed her hands up and down, back and forth until soap lather covered Drake's chest and abdomen. She slid her hands lower, down over and into his pubic hair. Soap slicked her first stroke down until she reached his cock.

"Ah Darlin'," Drake whispered. "I don't know how much more I can tolerate. Too much more and I'll ejaculate. I'll need a bit to recover."

"Cuddles are a wondrous part of recovering. Turn around. I'll get your back." Sara stroked upward toward Drake's waist. She closed the space between them, kissed his lips and lifted her hands. "Back please."

Drake faced away from her, giving her ample room to rub her soap-covered hands over his shoulders and down his back until she reached his ass. She stroked a bit lower until she cupped his ass cheek. "Firm. Nice. Makes me wonder how a swat or two on them would feel."

Drake turned partway back around. "Let's not. Not say we did either. Are you kinky?"

"No. Thanks for letting me know you aren't either. A little dominant and submissive play is okay at times." Sara turned, rinsed off and faced Drake. "Light bondage is okay too. Pain is not my pleasure."

Drake nodded as Sara moved past him. "Thanks for sharing." He stepped under the shower and began rinsing. "Maybe we need to talk more before we go further."

Sara exited the shower. Picking a towel up off the counter, she began drying off. "Mutual pleasure is important. Your pleasure is important. I'm definitely not kinky. Don't care pain is close to pleasure. Not my thing."

She wrapped the towel around her and faced Drake. "I've had enough pain in my life to last me many lifetimes over. I don't want or need it in my lovemaking."

Drake nodded. "Thanks for clarifying. I'll be out in a moment."

Sara faced the mirror. Her wet hair lay in clumps on her head. She needed to towel dry it and brush it out before she laid down. "I'll be right back. Need to brush my hair."

Drake peered around the shower curtain. The bathroom was empty. He turned the shower off and stepped out. As he reached for a towel, he wondered if they'd talk too much or not enough. Showering had taken longer than he expected. He snickered, looked up and let go a sigh. Sara wasn't back yet. How did he explain laughing at his own inanities? It was clear from their conversation neither of them was out for a quickie. One thing was clear. They took their time, touched, caressed and pleasured each other some. Uneasiness, shame or fear hadn't shown up. As he hung up his towel, Sara entered the bathroom. Sans her towel, working her brush through her hair as if she did this nude in front of him regularly. She was at ease. Drake leaned over and kissed Sara's shoulder.

"McGee is asleep. Teeth brushed, hair brushed, and I'm ready for loving cuddles." Sara faced Drake. "You?"

Drake picked up his toothbrush. "You're a step ahead of me. Five minutes and I'll be cuddling with you."

Sara laid her brush on the counter. "I'll get the bed ready, okay?"

"Sure." Drake held up his toothpaste-covered toothbrush, saluted her and started brushing.

Sara entered the bedroom. The glare of the overhead light brightly illuminated the room. She turned on one of the bedside lamps and clicked off the overhead light. A subdued glow filled the room forming a blurred at the edges circular area across the pillows and tops of the blanket and sheet. The softer cozier intimate impression focused on the two of them, not the stark show it all details the overhead light had. She placed the box of condoms on the nightstand closest to her. Sara stepped back, glanced around the room twice, and nodded. It'd been a while since she'd set the mood for passion, lovemaking, even sexual cuddles. Sounds of Drake gargling filtered out of the bathroom and into the bedroom. She smiled. He took care of himself, cared for himself as well as others, and made sure those he cared about knew it. Michael and Lindsay had pointed that out more than once and she'd seen it through his actions at the events they'd both been at.

Sara pulled back the covers and got into the bed. As she leaned back against the pillows, she smiled again. Her palms weren't sweaty. Her heart beat with a steady rhythm. Doubt and worry weren't present. Whatever happened next, she was sure of one thing. She was here because she wanted to be and Drake wanted her here too.

Drake rinsed his mouth one last time, hung the hand towel next to his towel, and turned off the light as he exited the bathroom. He paused at the edge of the doorway as he reached the bedroom. The prior glare of the overhead light was gone. Ambient lighting glowed off the walls and onto the bed creating a warm invitation. Sara lay back against the pillows, the sheet and blanket draped over her legs. She patted the bed next to her. "Come and join me."

"Is there enough room for two?" Drake sat on the edge of the bed close to Sara.

"Sure is. If you get in on the other side." Sara pointed to the empty space next to her.

"Nah, I prefer this way." Drake stretched one leg out on the bed, then his other and rolled partway on his side.

"You're going to fall off." Sara patted the part opposite her. "There's room here."

"Oh, I'm getting there. " Drake swung one leg over her. He rolled onto his knees, placed both hands on either side of her and winked. "Maybe this is where I need to be." He slowly stretched out until he lay on top of her. He laid his head on her close to her breasts.

Sara chafed her hand together, warming them. She laid her palms down on Drake's shoulders, pressing down as she massaged with small circular movements. "You worked so hard to get this far. My strong handsome sexy firemen."

Drake lifted his head, grinning. "There is that. And this. . ." His voice trailed off. He puckered his lips, pressed them against Sara and . . .

Sounds of a raspberry pfffft against skin rang out.

"St-stop," Sara giggled. Drake nibbled along her waist, tickling her first. "Not fair. That tickles."

Drake rolled off her onto the empty space beside her. "Well, depends. Found out you're ticklish. I got in the bed. And. . ." He yawned as he pulled the blanket and sheet over him.

"Too sleepy for more?" Sara asked, trailing her fingers down and over Drake's chest and abdomen.

Drake sucked in his stomach, snickered and winked. "No tickling."

"Why not? I haven't found your ticklish spot yet." Sara combed her fingertips through Drake's pubic hair.

"Thought you wanted this." Drake flipped on his side, looped an arm around her shoulders and nibbled her neck.

Drake nipped the spot beneath Sara's ear. Capturing her earlobe between his teeth, he suckled and nipped the flesh until Sara began squirming. He let go, pulling back. "I'd love to be doing that to your clit."

There was no mistaking Sara's reaction; she trembled from her shoulders down to her hip jerks.

Drake trailed nips followed by kisses and soothing laves down her neck until he reached her collarbone. He licked the slight indentation close to the base of her throat, pulled back more and blew across her wet flesh. Goosebumps, tingles, and desire flooded her. He cupped her breast with one hand, raised it, and suckled her nipple between his lips.

"Oh," Sara moaned. "You know my sweet spots."

Drake worried the tip of Sara's nipple with his teeth. He suckled once more and let go. "Finding your sweet spots is just the beginning. Your sweetest spot is here." He stroked down her waist, over her abdomen with his palm until he reached the apex of her mons. "Here is where your fire and heat reach out, drawing me into their embrace."

He rose up, leaned over Sara, and laid against her. Her pubic hair mixed with his. The core of their desire almost touching. Drake lowered himself to the point his forehead almost rested on Sara's. "A taste, a sampling of you before you and I join in the ride to a mutual orgasm."

CHAPTER SIXTEEN

O ther men had said similar words, used the same tactics, and barely scratched the surface of the fiery passion Drake ignited. Joined together riding the crest of the wave of a mutual orgasm sounded delicious. Tasting each other—Sara jerked again. Drake slipped one finger, then two into her wetness, thrusting them in and out, mimicking the age-old sexual dance two people did. He stroked in slowly finding her g-spot. Lightly over and around, slow then fast, until—Sara gripped Drake's arm.

"Much more and I'm going to orgasm hard. Do you want your taste?"

"Yes." Drake slid his hand out from between her legs.

"I want to taste you." Sara reached down, closing her fingers around him. She rubbed her palm over the head of his cock and down to his balls and back up twice. With each stroke up, she applied a small squeeze and release as she reached the tip of him. Wetness oozed out coating the tips of her fingers. She raised her hand, sniffed and scrutinized Drake. "Let's see if you're finger-licking good."

Sara puckered her lips and slid two fingers into her mouth. Salty, tang, and a rush of sweetness glided across her taste buds, lingering for a bit until she swallowed. "Hmm, delightful. How about a second taste?"

Drake held up his hand. "My turn." He slipped both fingers slick with Sara's wetness into his mouth. Hints of spiciness and salty greeted him. "Delicious." He yawned before he could say more.

Sara covered her mouth, trying to keep from yawning. "Are we too tired to do much more tonight?"

Drake shrugged and nodded. "I want to rock us to mutual pleasure and fall asleep in each other's arms afterwards."

"Agree." Sara reached for the box of condoms. "I want you."

Drake held out his hand palm up. "Let me put the condom on. Much more stimulation and I'm done for the evening."

Sara tore open the foil packet, took out the condom and laid it on Drake's hand. "I'm right behind you on the stimulation." She yawned again.

"Lay on your side with your back to me. I'll spoon to you and enter you from behind." Drake slowly eased the condom down and over his hardness. His balls were tight to him. He wasn't going to last long once he slipped into Sara.

Sara lay on her side, raised one leg, and reached back toward him. Drake scooted closer until his chest and stomach pressed against Sara's back and hips. He rocked forward. Her hand brushed over him close to the tip of his cock. He held still, not sure what to do. If the condom tore, he'd have to put another on. "Careful. Cup your hand around me and guide me in."

Sara reached back a bit further, waiting until Drake lay in her hand. "I've got you. I'm rocking back as you rock forward. In you go."

Bit by bit, Drake entered her with short thrusts. She lifted her leg up and back. Drake rocked forward again. . .

"You feel so good." Drake put his hand on her waist and started thrusting in and out in short bursts. "So warm."

"Hold still for a moment. Just soak in the feelings." Sara wet her lips, trying to find the words. Joined in the age-old dance of male and female mating. In and out. Back and forth. Yet, there was more. Parts of her reached out beyond her physical body, reaching upwards, seeking an oneness that came about when—"Sweet heaven, how did you know?"

Drake nipped her shoulder, kissed the nip mark and whispered. "Every part of you is pulsing. Your nipples, your clit, and where you cradle me, each warm, wonderful squeeze hugs me tighter and draws me into you."

Drake captured her nipple between his thumb and finger, plucking and squeezing. He reached between them, stroking until he reached her clit. Rapid quick circular strokes over and around.

Sara tried to speak. She couldn't. Words, coherent thoughts ceased. Her eyes closed as the coil deep inside her exploded. The first orgasmic blast washed up and over her like waves crashing upon the shore. Ebbs and short bursts combined together into a tidal wave pulling her deep into the bliss that a heart connection with the right person brought.

Drake let go of Sara's nipple. His balls tightened against him igniting an explosive inward surge that engulfed him from the inside out. All he could do was feel. Feel his jisim pump up and out. Orgasmic energy reached down into his groin sending wave after wave of intense pleasure throbbing through and over him until his heart cried out, *she's the one.*

"Oh my god," Drake murmured. "Wow. Someone help me back inside my body."

"As soon as I find mine." Sara clasped his hand. "That was intense."

"Mind-boggling intense." Drake heaved a deep sigh. "We set ourselves on fire."

"We connected, ignited and ...." Sara licked her lips. "BOOM!"

"Yup, boom!' Drake pulled his hand away from Sara's. "Hold still for a moment. I want to be sure the condom doesn't come off as I pull out."

"Thank you, Drake. I appreciate your thoughtfulness." Sara lifted her leg. "Ready when you are."

Drake carefully encircled his cock below the top of the condom with his hand. Rocking back slowly, he withdrew until he lay beside Sara once again. "Okay, I'm out."

Sara lowered her leg and sat up. "Whew. I'm ready to sleep. I'm going to the bathroom. Be right back."

Drake nodded, even though his eyes threatened to close. He knew he couldn't doze off until he checked the condom. Even a minute possible tear could mean a pregnancy. His Granny's words echoed through his mind. *Be safe. Be smart. Be ready for your children.*

He rolled to his side, still holding on to the condom. How did he get out of the bed without making a mess?

"I think you can use this." Sara held out a wet washcloth. "It's warm. Do you need help getting the condom off?"

"Kinda." Drake scooted toward Sara, still holding on to his cock and the condom with both hands. "Wrap the washcloth around and over me and the condom. We'll work the condom and washcloth off me at the same time."

Sara gradually wrapped the washcloth around him. Softly touching him as she did. "Ready when you are."

"Not too fast. I'm letting go now." He lowered his hands and blew Sara a kiss. "You're in control."

"Okay, here we go." Sara worked her hands steadily down him until she had the condom and washcloth bunched around the tip of him. She glanced at him.

Drake nodded. He reached up, grasped himself close to Sara's hands. "Off it all comes."

Sara stepped back, the bunched washcloth and condom in her hands. Drake rolled to the edge of the bed, stood up, and held his hand out. "Thank you for helping. I've got it from here."

Sara shook her head. "I'd like to know together if the condom held up." She exited the bedroom, holding her hands out in front of her.

Drake followed. Tonight Sara had entered his heart in ways no other woman had. Her determination, her care, and resolve that both of them were in the outcome together. Partnering was important.

Sara spread the washcloth out on the bathroom counter. She stepped to the side, giving Drake room to stand beside her. "You take one edge. I'll take the other. Together we'll find out."

Drake picked up the edge opposite her. "On three. One."

"Two," Sara said, raising her hand level with Drake's

"Three," Drake said, raising his side to eye level.

In the reservoir tip, there was a small pool of his jisim. "Shall we see if it holds water?"

"Is that necessary?" Sara asked, running her fingers over the washcloth. "It doesn't feel sticky."

"To be on the safe side, I say yeah." Drake turned on a trickle of water. "You can let go. I'll hold it under the water."

Sara moved closer to him as he began filling the condom. No water dripped out of the tip or sides as the condom filled. She kissed his cheek. "Thank you for understanding, caring and being here."

Drake emptied the condom, wrapped it in toilet paper and dropped it in the wastebasket. "You're welcome. Both of us needed to know there wasn't an oops tonight."

"Now we can sleep without worrying." Sara yawned, reaching for his hand.

"Yes, we can." Drake clasped Sara's hand as they exited the bathroom.

Drake sat on the end of the bed. "Together or apart?"

"Are you asking if I'm staying or retreating?" Sara sat next to him. "If you are, my answer is I'm staying. I'm not walking away or hiding. You?"

Drake rose, faced her. "I'm staying. Fear engulfed me for a moment. Sorry."

"Nothing to be sorry about. We're in new territory. Out of our comfort individual comfort zones." Sara stood, closed the space between them, wrapping her arms around Drake. "We've created a new comfort zone the embraces us. I like that."

"Yes, together we've expanded our comfort zone to include both of us." Drake embraced her and brushed his lips over hers. "Side of the bed choice?"

"Snuggled with you is my choice. Yours?" Sara moved to the head of the bed, straightening the blanket and sheet. She turned back the covers, patted the bed and held her hand out.

"Snuggled with you too. Outside edge is my preference. Habit from sleeping at the station." Drake squeezed her hand and let go.

Sara lay down, turned on her side and worked her way to the middle of the bed. She held up the covers and patted the space next to her. "If you need more space, let me know."

Drake turned the bedside lamp off, settled in beside her, spooning to her, and pulled the covers over both of them.

Quiet filled the house as sleep claimed them. Outside in the cloudless sky, one star almost directly over the house shined brightly as if the powers-that-be watched over the occupants inside.

CHAPTER SEVENTEEN

Saturday Morning

S
ara rolled over, reached out, and—nothing. Her hand fell to the cool mattress. She opened her eyes, blinked and sat up. Where was Drake?

"Drake," she called out, flinging off the covers. His spot was cool, almost cold. How long had he been gone? Was he okay?

She ran into the hall. Silence. No running water. No sounds. Maybe he was in her bathroom?

More silence. "Drake," she called again. Barks and yips sounded. McGee was still in his crate. He'd walked out? Why? What had gone wrong? Sara ran into her bedroom, grabbed her robe off the back of her bedroom door and turned. A bright yellow sheet stuck to her mirror caught her attention. She stepped into her slippers as she crossed the room. As she reached the dresser, she shoved her hands into the pockets on her robe. She leaned forward and read the first line aloud.

Dearest Sara,

I'd rather be snuggled with you under the covers cuddling than at work. Michael called as I let McGee out for his morning potty run. Seems I've got decorating duty and overseeing food delivery for tonight's party. At least I get to wear jeans. I'll be back around five to shower and change into my work uniform.

Last night was wonderful. Saying thank you doesn't feel right when there is so much more I want to tell you in person. There's homemade pancakes and bacon in the fridge. Sorry, I can't be there to enjoy them with you. Coffee maker is ready to go just turn it on.

Until 5 P.M., my dear,
Drake
XXOO

Sara grasped the paper, pulling it off the mirror. Part of her tingled with joy. He'd left a note. . . not a just a note—he'd left a love note. She dropped down on the edge of the bed, still holding the paper. Her psyche demanded analysis of the missive and scrutiny of every word nuance and pen stroke. She folded the paper in half. Reading more into what was there made no sense. Feeding her past fear and worry promoted nothing but unfounded fear and angst.

McGee barked and yipped as he scratched at the door of the crate. Sara rose. Tonight would be the first time she and Drake went out as a couple. She glanced at the clock on her nightstand. 10:15 A.M. She had almost seven hours to decide what to wear, bake the cake she'd signed up for for the funding raising auction, and TLC herself.

"All right, McGee." Sara opened the crate. "Come on, let's go downstairs."

McGee raced out of the bedroom. Sara followed, picking up her pace as she reached the stairs. McGee was down them and heading toward the kitchen. As she reached the bottom of the stairs, she paused. Drake's work uniform lay draped over the banister. He would need time to iron it when he got back. The dance and party started at seven-thirty. Not much time for him to shower, dress and press his uniform.

Sara held up the uniform shirt, gazed at Drake's name badge and medals. One was for community service. Another for outstanding performance and the next two signified his rank and tenure with Peyton Corners' fire department; emergency medical technician paramedic and six years on the job. The last signified his other job, fire safety inspector. She picked up the uniform pants and continued into the kitchen. McGee paced by the back door, stopped and started to lift his leg.

"No, you don't." Sara tossed the uniform on a chair and rushed to the door. She stepped around McGee, opened the door, and glared down at him. "You know better. Out you go."

McGee barked and ran out the door. A burst of cold air whipped around the door, twirling around her ankles, and reaching higher chilling places she hadn't planned on exposing to cold winds. She shoved the door shut and went back to the table. She pressed her lips together as she ran her hand over Drake's uniform. Twice in the night, she'd awoken. Heard him mutter in his sleep. Danger wasn't far from his thoughts or dreams. Life came with ups and downs. Nothing was guaranteed. Her conscience echoed the one question her heart already knew the answer to. Was she turning back instead of looking forward? Moving away from this chance at love?

Sara drew back her hand. She turned and walked away from the cloud of doubt and dismay threatening to envelop her. Past experiences left their mark. She had choices. The one she was making was not looking back. She was looking and moving forward. Drake and she deserved a chance. She was making sure they got it.

She turned on the coffee maker, opened the cabinet above it and took out one of her cookbooks. The peaches and cream crumble layer cake would take a couple of hours to make. She glanced out the window as she laid the cookbook on the counter. McGee raced toward the door as if the wind and he were racing.

She called out as she opened the door. "It's McGee in the home stretch."

McGee ran inside and streaked by her, heading for the living room. Sara quickly shut the door. She walked into the living room. McGee sat on the couch, huddled between two pillows. "McGee, you beat the wind. Yeah, you."

She started up the steps, planning her day. Coffee and food would keep until she dressed and came back downstairs. She hoped Drake got a chance to eat before he started decorating.

Drake laid his egg and cheese croissant down, picked up his large take-out cup of coffee, and sipped. The southwestern spices and the pepper and colby jack cheese mix combo usually tasted great. But. . .it's wasn't homemade maple and nutmeg hotcakes and extra crispy bacon with Sara. He hoped she saw the note he'd left attached to her mirror. McGee had been on his best behavior. He settled back down in the crate after his potty run and a couple of biscuits.

Damn it, he and Sara should have woken up together. Snuggle more and maybe made love again. The L word. Well, last night wasn't wham bam thank you did and done. Each of their orgasms was intense. Neither of them could speak for several moments. They'd laid in each other's arms, blissfully reposed, trying to find their way back into their bodies. Somewhere in the ether, their hearts had entwined, coupled, and separated. Last night was like meeting an old lover again, and yet it was new, different, and unique.

"Hey Drake," Michael called, walking past him. "You might wanna drink more of that coffee. We got decorations to hang. You got ladder duty."

"Wait, how did I get that?" Drake gulped a swallow of his lukewarm coffee.

"You volunteered. I asked you before I ran to Lemuel's to pick up our breakfast order, where did you want to help. You said you'd help with the ladder detail." Michael laughed as he walked back by him. "You can be on top of it hanging crepe paper or down below, moving it along and making sure it stays steady."

Drake broke off a hunk of his croissant, stuffed it in his mouth, chewed and washed it down with a gulp of coffee. He glanced at the ladder and up to the ceiling. He didn't fear heights. Somehow straddling the top of that ladder with a staple gun in one hand and a roll of crepe paper in his other didn't feel like something he was ready to tackle. Maybe after his second or third cup of coffee. He yawned. He'd slept deep and solid for the six hours and then another two until his bladder nudged him awake again. Tonight, he planned on getting to sleep early or at least snuggling early with Sara. Nothing said they had to stay until the last dance was over.

"Who's working with me?" Drake called out, recapping his coffee cup. The sooner he and his crepe partner got done, the sooner he could finish his breakfast. Probably would be his lunch knowing Michael and his last minute details. Drake chuckled as Frank approached clutching a bag with red and green crepe paper and a staple gun. Frank held them out away from him as if they were poison or set to bite him.

"Okay, Drake. Staples all ready for you to start hanging." Frank's cheesy grin said what he didn't. He didn't want to be on top of the ladder any more than Drake did.

"No, you got the longer arms. You are hanging and I'm steadying." Drake walked over to the stepladder center of the room. "Someone has to make sure you are doing okay up there. I'm the one."

Frank muttered as he climbed the ladder, the bag of crepe paper hanging from his belt and the staple gun in one hand. Close to the top of the ladder, Frank stopped, looked down and shook his head. "Now I know why they tell us don't look down in training. It's a long damn way down there."

He stuck his tongue out, blew a raspberry and finished climbing the ladder. Drake chuckled as he steadied the ladder. His turn climbing and hanging was coming. Michael had to point that out as he walked back toward the community center entrance. Drake glanced at his watch as Frank stepped off the ladder. 12 P.M. At this rate of up and down the ladder and stapling, it would take them hours to hang the damn crepe paper. Frank reached for the ladder to move it to the next spot.

"Hang on, Frank. Joe and Nelson are done setting up the tables. I think with the four of us doing this we can get it done quicker." Drake walked over to where Joe and Nelson stood. "Nelson, do you think your brother will let us borrow two of his cherry pickers for the afternoon?"

"He might. Let me call him and find out." Nelson pulled his cell phone out and stepped outside.

"Joe, how many staple guns did Michael bring with him?" Drake tipped his head back and started pacing the length of the room. Joe followed him, matching his pace by pace.

"Three staple guns. Why?" Joe held up seven fingers. "I counted seven paces. My pace is thirty-six inches wide."

"That's what I got. If Nelson's brother lets us use the cherry pickers, With two of us in each one, we could hang the crepe paper quicker and easier." Drake walked back to where Frank stood. "Hope Nelson can get the larger ones. That will allow us to work in tandem."

Frank nodded. "Good idea. Meanwhile I'm going to finish my coffee."

Twenty minutes later, Nelson and his brother drove two cherry pickers through the community center double doors. Michael was right behind them. He gave Drake two thumbs up and a pat on the shoulder.

Laughter followed as Drake, Joe, Frank and Nelson drove the cherry pickers around the room trying to avoid bumping into each other. Their movement and driving resembled carnival bumper cars.

"Frank and I will take the east-west sections. Joe, you and Nelson take north-south." Drake held up his staple gun and bag of crepe paper. "Ready set go."

Sounds of staples ejecting and slow-moving motors sounded. More laughter followed. Suggestions on how best to twist and drape the crepe paper arose. Two hours later, the teams lowered the cherry pickers and stepped out. Greens and reds intertwined across the ceiling, interspersed with golds and silvers.

Drake sat next to Frank at one of the tables, saluted him with his cold coffee and grinned. Joe and Nelson pulled chairs up to the table. The four high-fived each other and picked up their half-finished breakfast croissants.

"I hope Michael doesn't expect us to work through lunch." Drake wiped his mouth. "He better have food ready. We're due back at the station in twenty minutes. Someone mentioned chili right before we left."

Nelson held up his hand. "We keep eating like this and we won't want to eat tonight."

"Don't believe it. We've got cleaning duty back at the station. That will keep us busy and work off breakfast and lunch." Frank picked up their trash and started toward the door. "We best be on our way."

Drake glanced around the center again. Later a small decorated tree would fill the corner close to where Santa would sit, handing out small gifts to the children attending. Families would start arriving around seven for the catered meal. Some would bring dishes to share. The dance would begin around nine after the cake auction finished. Had Sara signed up for the cake auction? Was she bringing a dish to share?

He patted the pocket of his jeans. The small box he'd grabbed from his place was nestled in his pocket. He hoped the night finished out with the promises his dreams and heart had shown him as he slept.

CHAPTER EIGHTEEN

Saturday Late Afternoon

Sara folded the newspaper and laid it on the table next to her empty breakfast plate. The sink was full of mixing bowls, measuring cups and spoons. The first cake pan sat on the counter cooling. The second had forty more minutes to go. Next to the first cake pan, the crockpot cooled. The roast she'd put on three hours ago was done. Ready to shred and mix with her signature Louisiana barbecue sauce. She'd added the left-over juice from the jalapenos Drake had brought over. Fiery, tangy, and sweet. Just the way she was feeling after eating, two cups of coffee, and a snack-filled lunch. As she stood, she caught a glimpse of her reflection in the window over the sink. Her hair stood up in places. Flour covered parts of her top and cheeks.

"I look like I wrestled a fifty-pound bag of flour instead of emptying a one-pound one." She rinsed her plate and cup, placed them in the dishwasher along with the bowls and measuring cups and spoons and turned it on. Sara washed her hands and dried them. The oven timer showed thirty minutes until the second cake was done. She had enough time to shred the roast and let it marinate in the barbecue sauce.

Laying the roast on the large wooden cutting board, Sara sliced the roast in half. She cut the halves into quarters and kept trimming each section until the entire roast was small chunks. Steam rose off the pile of meat. She glanced at the oven timer. Less than twenty minutes until the second cake was done. From the fridge, she took out the basic sauce she'd prepared earlier. The crockpot's warmth would help the sauce penetrate the meat and mix with the roast's seasonings. A layer at a time, she added sauce, then meat and stirred until the crockpot was full. As she dried her hands, the oven timer beeped.

Sara turned the oven off and set the second cake pan close to the first. The peach cream cheese frosting along with the graham cracker and peaches filling was done. Putting the cake together wouldn't take more than fifteen to twenty minutes. The second layer needed about fifteen minutes more to finish cooling before she could put the cake together. She glanced at the kitchen clock. She had about ninety minutes until Drake returned. Time enough to choose her outfit, shower, leisurely dress, and take his pressed uniform upstairs.

As she exited the laundry room carrying the hanger with Drake's uniform on it, Sara glanced around the kitchen. There was a difference to it. The atmosphere didn't feel lonely, silent, and empty. Drake's presence filled it. Knowing he would be back soon. Knowing he wanted to be here. Knowing he cared. . .her heart beat faster as she mouthed the word her heart and psyche had chimed since their sexual and ethereal joining last night. The L word rolled off her lips into the air. Could she—would she—admit it aloud? To herself, possibly. To Drake, she wasn't sure.

Sara carefully draped Drake's uniform over one arm and started up the stairs. What would she wear tonight? The cold air that followed McGee in took wearing her favorite dress off the list. Images of color combinations flared and faded. One-color kept coming back, periwinkle blue. The sky-toned hue that she'd fallen in love with during her summer beach vacations. The marine blue of the water as she gazed out across the bay from her hotel room balcony her first morning in Hawaii. Yes, she'd fallen in love with blue. Maybe a splash of yellow and mauve. She had time to compare tops and sweaters after she showered.

Drake sat down next to Michael at the table in the station's dining room. "I know you and Lindsay tried to pair up anyone attending solo."

"Yes, we did. It didn't work out as good as we thought it might." Michael sipped his coffee. "Why do you bring this up?"

"Well, Sara and I are attending together. Our connection sparked ahead of the dance." Drake peeled the paper back on his cupcake and bit into it. Chocolate and salted caramel. Gooeyness, salty tang and sweet rolled across his tongue as he chewed.

"Care to explain?" Michael saluted him with his coffee mug. "I got time to listen."

Drake laughed. "You want to know how and when so you can tell Lindsay. I don't kiss and tell. Don't even boast, brag or gossip."

"Lindsay is going to bug me until she finds out. Come on. Give me something to tell her." Michael reached for a cupcake.

Drake downed the last of his coffee. "Neighbors help each other out. That's all I'm saying. Now when do we unload the food trucks?"

Michael nudged him, grinning. "That ain't a tidbit."

Drake shook his head. "It's a clue and you gotta think about it. Subject is food trucks."

"All right," Michael wiped his hands and mouth on a napkin and stood. "Trucks arrive at the center around five-forty-five. Most of the food will be hot and ready to put out on the table. The service staff arrives at five-thirty. Lindsay and Sara are in charge of setting up the cake auction area."

Drake glanced at his watch as he rose. "I'd better get a move on. It's 4:30. I'll be back around 6 to help with the food set up."

Michael picked up both their mugs. "See you then. Tell Sara, Lindsay is going to want full disclosure."

"I doubt Sara is the kiss and tell type either. Besides, how would it look if the station chief was blushing or his mouth hanging open?" Drake waved and kept walking. Michael would have some smartass comeback. He couldn't blurt it out without the crew hearing him. Drake chuckled as he reached the exit. Score Drake one hundred. Michael zip.

Drake zipped his jacket and pulled his watch cap on. He shielded his eyes as he walked out the door. The afternoon sun set low in the sky. Reds, oranges, and golden hues streaked the clouds and sky. The afternoon warmth was waning. Some of the snow had melted. Drifts and patches of ice remained. Some said a white Christmas brought good luck and heralded a new year of joy and opportunities. He patted his jeans pocket as he unlocked the truck door. He hoped the box in his pocket brought the same glow and sparkle to Sara's smile and eyes. A gift straight from the heart said a lot. His other gift would add to the Christmas cheer he planned on spreading tonight. He clicked on the radio as he put the truck into gear. A familiar one from his high school years started. Drake smiled as he sang along. Instead of the line about mom smooching Santa Claus, he sang about Sara hugging and kissing Santa Claus. He chuckled as more risqué lyrics came to mind. As he pulled up to the stoplight, he made sure the windows were closed. He didn't need to try to explain to the police why he was signing naughty songs so loud.

Sara stepped out of the shower. Condensation fogged the mirror. She used one end of her towel to wipe part of the mirror off. A slight flush tinged her cheeks and neck. Part was due to the heat of the shower. The majority was her thoughts. Memories of last night flooded through her the moment she stepped into the shower. Drake's presence lingered everywhere she looked or touched. Her view and world had changed. Others had touched her, but not deep in her heart and psyche like Drake did. The first time she paid attention, gave him the once-over female assessment was during the times he tossed the ball for McGee. A simple thing. Not one her neighbor had to do. Drake did though. Retrieved McGee's ball from where it was wedged between two fence posts and tossed it back into the yard for him. McGee had chased the ball and run back with it to the spot, nosing it back between the posts. The two had played fetch for forty minutes.

Drake offered help each time he was out in the yard. They'd had brief conversations. Yet, somewhere inside, she'd known for a while he was special. She hadn't realized how special and magical their connection was until they touched more than in a physical way. Their souls and hearts touched, embraced and bonded last night. The spark that lit the candle inside her heart drove out all the fear and anxiety she'd hid behind. Could she explain this to Drake? One word flashed through her mind. The L word. Maybe it was time to listen openheartedly to her heart and embrace what was before her.

Sara wrapped the bath sheet around her and exited the bathroom. On her bed lay two possible outfits. A periwinkle blue vest she'd crocheted, dark brown slacks, and a gold-colored turtleneck. The other consisted of dark blue slacks, a red blouse, and a cardigan she made out of a three-tone variegated yarn. The cashmere yarn had caught her eye six months prior. She'd bought it out of the mark-down bin and tucked it away, saving it for a special item. Going through a box of older patterns, she came across the pattern her grandmother had given her for her first complex project. Working the yarn into a simple cardigan had turned into a self-love project that had seen her through some of her loneliest periods. Had she finished it because she was ready to emerge from her cocoon of loneliness and open herself up to new possibilities? Tonight might be the beginning of something wonderful and great.

Blues and yellows reminded her of spring. The partially melted snow and ice. . .cold and wet. That wasn't the effect she wanted to inspire. Warm, cozy, and approachable without sending out more signals than what was needed to get Drake's attention. As she put on her bra and panties, she glanced out the window. The last rays of the setting sun reached in, briefly touched her and disappeared. Tonight's forecast called for more snow. The temperature would drop drastically as darkness fell. Sensible shoes and warm clothes guided her choices.

She sat down on the bed, pulled on her trouser socks, and reached for the closest pair of pants. Brown, gold, and a mixture of mauve, beige, and two-tone blue were her choices. She tucked the turtleneck into the waist of her pants and threaded a belt through the belt loops. As she reached for one of her hikers, McGee rushed out of the bedroom, excitedly barking. Drake was home.

Sara smiled as she finished tying her hikers. She stood, walked to her dresser, and opened her jewelry box. She opened the center compartment. Inside was the silver two-toned barrette she'd picked up at an antique shop in Nashville. She brushed her hair, divided it into three sections starting at the base of her head with the French braid. Holding the end of the braid in one hand, she secured the end of the braid with the barrette. The end of the braid draped over her shoulder adding a bit of glitter to her outfit. She hoped Drake approved of her choices.

CHAPTER NINETEEN

Saturday Evening

"Hey McGee," Drake called out as he shrugged out of his jacket. He leaned down, reached toward McGee. McGee sniffed his hand, backed up, barked, and nuzzled his hand. "Yeah, you smell Smokey from down at the station. How about my other hand? I only petted Smokey with one hand."

Drake held out his other hand. McGee sniffed both hands, nuzzled them and moved closer to him. "All right, buddy. Maybe I need to wash my hands, then pet you."

McGee whined and cuddled tighter to Drake. Drake chuckled. "Okay. I guess Smokey smells good. But I need to shower and change. So get your pets now or not until after Sara and I get back."

"He better get them now. If the dance runs as late as Lindsay said it's supposed to we won't be home until very late. Cathy and Boris are watching McGee for the evening."

Drake squatted down next to McGee. "Now you be a good boy. Mind your manners and don't tease Boris too much. Go to bed when Cathy tells you too and only a couple of treats. Okay?"

McGee stood up on his hind legs, tail wagging and licked Drake's face. McGee barked and ran off toward the kitchen. Sara laughed. "You said the magic word. You gotta give him a treat and a potty run while I get his overnight tote ready."

"Sara," Drake said, straightening. "Got a moment?"

Sara moved closer. "Sure. What's up?"

Drake slipped an arm around Sara's waist, hugged her to him, and pressed his lips against hers. He started to pull back.

"More," Sara whispered, bunching his hair between her fingers.

"Certainly," Drake murmured, pulling Sara tighter to him. "More is a good thing."

Sara's lips met his. The tip of her tongue traced his bottom lip. He parted his lips, his tongue meeting hers. Tastes, sips, and flashes of their day chased across their taste buds as they mated with their mouths. Tightly pressed together, neither noticed their chaperone intently watching them. McGee cocked his head left and right. His tail wagging so quickly, he scooted himself several inches from the door. He yipped and whined, then as if on cue from the powers that be, he started barking.

Drake broke off the kiss first. "Wow," he whispered, tilting his head back. "I think our chaperone saved us."

"Saved us?" Sara asked, inhaling and exhaling rapidly.

"Uh, yeah." Drake moved back, letting air in where their heated bodies permitted none moments before. "My mind was on a repeat of last night."

Sara nodded. "Me too."

Drake turned, walked over to the cabinets, took out the treat box, and shook one out. "I believe our chaperone deserves two. But we haven't got time for that."

Sara pointed at the door. "Give it to McGee when he comes back in. I'm going to get his overnight tote and coat."

Drake laid the treat on the counter, opened the door, and leaned down. "McGee, you need go potty. Then it's time to go see Boris."

Boris' deep bark sounded as McGee raced out the door. Drake smiled as McGee and Boris met at the fence. Soon woofs and barks sounded like two friends greeting each other.

Drake shut the door and made his way to the laundry room. His uniform wasn't there. He opened the washer and dryer. His laundry wasn't there either. He didn't remember taking it upstairs. "Sara," he called out, exiting the laundry room. "Did I take my—"

"Up here," Sara replied. Drake exited the kitchen and entered the living room. Sara stood at the top of the stairs holding a hanger with his ironed uniform on it.

"Sweetie, you didn't have to do that." Drake bounded up the stairs two at a time.

"I did it because I wanted to. Your clean folded laundry is in a basket on your bed. Clean sheets too." Sara held his uniform out to him.

"One moment." Drake entered his room. The bed was made up. The basket of laundry sat on one side of the bed. He turned. Sara stood at the edge of the doorway, holding the hanger with his uniform away from her. He walked over, took hold of the hanger and tugged. Sara stumbled into the room, stopping close to him. "Thank you for the gift. I appreciate this. Active partnering doesn't always need words. I like how we partner. Speaking of partnering, I need to go fetch McGee. "

"Not necessary," Sara kissed Drake's cheek. "I've got his tote bag ready to go. Cathy's meeting me at the back gate. Go ahead and get ready. I'll be in the kitchen finishing up the cake."

"Thanks again, hon. I won't be long. I'll help you pack up the cake and the barbecue pork." Drake hung the hanger on the edge of the closet doorframe. "By the way, you smell and look delicious."

Sara grinned and ducked her head. "Thanks. I gotta go deliver our chaperone to his sitter. If I stay here, we aren't going to make the dance. We don't need the entire station coming to check on us."

Drake laughed. "True. Besides, I need to shower and dress. If you stick around I might undress you too. Then we'd be delayed delivering McGee and getting things packed up."

He kissed Sara on the lips and trotted into the bathroom, clicking the door shut behind him.

Sara pressed her hand to her lips. She was smiling. Joyous banter and loving touches had happened. Yes, loving was the word. She could say it, admit it, and embrace the wonderful feeling coursing through her. She wrapped her arms around herself, tightened them and released. Not a motion or action of fear. Hugging herself felt good. Now she needed to get McGee delivered.

She pulled on her coat and picked up McGee's tote. As she reached the back door, she tucked the box of treats into the bag and pocketed the loose one. McGee and Boris would tussle and play until they wore each other out. Cathy's husband had offered to take Boris and McGee to the dog park tomorrow. Cathy had told her take him up on the offer. Their five-year-old twin nephews were visiting and the outing would tucker the quad out. Sara waved as she neared the back gate. Cathy already held a squirming McGee.

"What did he do now?" Sara asked, reaching into her pocket for the loose treat.

"Nothing. He wanted to chase Mrs. Nelson's cat. Boris already treed the poor thing twice. McGee doesn't need to take on one pissed-off pussy cat." Cathy held one hand out.

Sara handed Cathy the tote. "Well, McGee," Sara began shaking a finger at him. "I don't know if you deserve this." She held up the treat. McGee barked and squirmed more. "I'll let Cathy give you this so you leave Mrs. Nelson's cat alone."

"Come by when you're ready to get him tomorrow. No rush. Enjoy the dance." Cathy pocketed the treat and entered her house.

Sara shook her head as she entered the kitchen. Tonight she and Drake could do what they wanted. Stay out late, stay up all night, get frisky or ....Sara laughed. They could sleep in. Wow, what an amazing thing. Maybe she needed to let Boris and McGee have overnights more often. She laughed again as she hung up her coat. She hadn't laughed this much in a long time. It felt good. Joy brought its own rewards. It multiplied as personal perceptions changed. As she took out the icing and peach graham cracker filling from the fridge, she paused. She'd been humming. Humming a quirky ditty her granddad used to sing as he rocked her to sleep when she was sick. The song talked about loving the green frog hiding inside everyone. The frog thought he was the only one. He hid and refused to croak until one day someone challenged everyone to sing. To show their beauty with their voice. Everyone's frog sang out and in that moment, everyone found their own inner beauty. Sara knuckled away the tear trickling down her cheek. She'd hidden her frog, deep inside, hidden away from herself until now. She and her frog weren't hiding anymore. She was ready to tell Drake how she felt. What she knew deep in her heart. Was he ready to hear what she had to say?

Drake pulled back the shower curtain. Some days he wondered if he could ever take longer than ten minutes to shower. Standing under the shower using up hot water meant higher utility bills. He'd rather soak in his hot tub or take a lukewarm bath. He grinned as he toweled off. Images of his grandmother shaking the utility bill at him and asking him if he had extra cash to pay it flashed through his mind. His grandmother had stashed the money away, surprising him with a check that Christmas. The money had bought him his first car. The ride he needed to attend college and get back and forth to work. That Christmas was one of his favorites. His grandparents had given him several gifts that year. One was a piece of family history. As he hung up his towel, he glanced at his watch. 5:45 P.M. Crap, he better hurry up if he wanted time to talk with Sara before they left. Was she ready to hear what his heart had to say?

CHAPTER TWENTY

Drake entered the kitchen twenty minutes later. Sara turned toward him, smiling. Some smiles never made it to a person's lips. Some added a glow to the person's face. There was no mistaking Sara's smile. The slight flush on her cheeks, and the twinkle in her eyes as her gaze met his indicated she was genuinely happy to see him. Doubt could be a nasty predator. One that he wrestled with more than he liked. Reading others was never easy. He went with his gut and did the best he could. His gut and heart cheered the closer he got to Sara. Her smile didn't fade or change.

"Sorry, it took me longer." Drake reached for the cake carrier.

"No problem. I just finished putting the cake together. It needs about ten minutes to set before we pack it up. The crockpot is cool. We can get the pork ready to go." Sara put the knife and icing bowls in the sink. "The container is next to the crockpot."

Drake lifted the lid off the crockpot. Scents of tomato, jalapenos, and spices rushed up to greet him. "That smells awesome. I hope there's leftovers."

"I put some back for us in the fridge." Sara picked up a spoon. "Hold up the crockpot, please."

They worked in tandem, getting the sauce and pork into the container. Drake set the crockpot on the counter. "Sara, there's something I want to ask you."

Sara dumped water into the crockpot and faced him. "Okay."

"How do you feel about presents?" Drake washed and dried his hands.

"They're okay. Why do you ask?" Sara put the pork container into the tote she'd placed on the table.

"Some don't like exchanging presents. They feel obligated to. You're okay if I got you a Christmas present? Maybe two?" Drake picked up the tote and started toward the living room. "Do you need help packing the cake?"

"Gift exchanges are okay. I got you a couple things too." Sara closed the cake carrier and handed it to Drake. She got her coat from by the back door. "Cake is packed. You ready to go?"

"Yes, ready to go." Drake set the tote and the cake carrier on the coffee table and reached for his jacket. "Wait till Christmas morning to exchange?"

Sara chuckled. "If you like. It's only a few days off."

Drake put on his jacket and watch cap. "I'll drive. I'm good for Christmas eve or morning for gifts."

Sara wrapped her scarf around her neck and buttoned up her coat. As she put her hat on, she faced him. "Let's play it by ear. It's McGee and us. We can take it easy and leisurely enjoy the holiday."

"All right," Drake picked up the tote and the cake carrier. "Ready to go?"

"Yes." Sara took her keys out of her purse and locked the door. "I hope you're hungry. Several restaurants contributed food for tonight's potluck dinner sales. "

"I get to scope out the best entrees as I help unload the food." Drake opened the truck's passenger door. "I'll hand these to you once you're in."

Sara set the tote on the floor next to her purse "I'll hold the cake carrier on my lap."

Drake shut the door and sprinted around the truck. He set the cake carrier on the seat and got in. He fastened his seatbelt and turned toward Sara. "I'll hand you the cake carrier after you fasten your seatbelt. Safety first."

The click of Sara fastening her seatbelt sounded. "Done." She reached for the cake carrier. Her hand touched Drake's. He cupped his hand around hers, slightly squeezed and let go.

"Reach a bit lower and you've got the hand of the carrier." Drake started the truck and backed up. "Glad McGee is overnighting with Boris. We don't have to hurry home. Maybe we can catch the stars from Lookout Point on the way home."

"I can think of a better place. We can see the stars from my bedroom window if I open the curtains. Nice warm comforter and fluffy pillows. Better than sitting in the cold." Sara patted his arm. "Besides, maybe we'll need another shower after the dance."

Drake rubbed his lips together, swallowed and opened his mouth to speak. Words failed him. No come back would do. The images flashing through his mind were very vivid and repeats from last night. He gripped the steering wheel tighter as he put the truck into gear. If he heard Sara right, he just got propositioned. And his answer was *yes*!

"We're off to the community fundraiser and dance." Drake glanced at Sara as she glanced at him. "I've got me an awesome date. Thanks for going with me."

Sara nodded. "Me too. Awesome date. Hunkish guy. And one heck of a lover."

Drake forced his mind to focus on his driving and not the thoughts his horny id and ego were pumping through his mind.

Forty minutes later, they pulled into the community center's parking lot. Michael, Joe and Frank stood near the back of one of the food trucks. Nelson was helping unload another. Drake parked close to Michael's car.

"I'll take the tote in and check with Lindsay where she wants it. Are you okay with the cake carrier?" Drake got out.

"Yes. Go on. I know you need to help unload. I'll help Lindsay finish setting up." Sara got out, holding the cake carrier.

Drake rushed inside, handed Lindsay the tote and rushed back outside. Michael held up his hands as he approached. "Slow down. Don't need you slipping on any ice patches. Help Nelson unload the Farmer's Pavilion truck. Lindsay mentioned needing help setting up more tables. More food and folks than anticipated. Seems a lot of folks are turning out."

"Another reason why I love living in Peyton Corners. The community comes together in support of those around them. They help as they can and give back. I'll see what Nelson needs help with." Drake walked over to where Nelson and the owner of Farmers Pavilion stood.

"Hi, Drake. I'm Caleb Sewald, Angela's brother. Glad to meet you." Caleb held his handout.

Drake grasped Caleb's hand firmly and shook it. "Angela mentioned you were moving to town last time I was over. Pleasure to meet you."

"Parker told me I might meet you tonight. He and Angela will be here later. They're picking up my fiancée Izzy and our parents at the airport in Chattanooga." Caleb climbed into the back of the truck and handed out several trays of fresh fruits and vegetables. Drake and Nelson loaded the trays onto tiered serving carts and rolled them inside.

Caleb jumped out of the back of the truck. "That does it. I'll be back in a while. I appreciate the help." Caleb closed up the back of the truck. "Looking forward to sampling some of the food, enjoying the music and taking home some of those baked goods."

"You're welcome," Nelson said. "I'll check with Michael if anyone else needs help out here."

Drake walked around to the front of the truck with Caleb. "I hope your family's flight gets in okay. I bet Angela is happy to have you here for Christmas."

"She sure is. Mom and Dad wanted to surprise them, but Izzy beat them to the punch. I'll let you in on a surprise for Angela and Parker." Caleb got in the truck.

"I'll keep my lip zipped." Drake drew his finger across his lips.

Caleb chuckled. "Mom and Dad are staying until Angela delivers. They might sell the bed and breakfast to our cousin and move to Peyton Corners."

Drake let out a low whistle. "Wonder how Parker is going to handle having his in-laws so close."

Caleb shook his head. "He's still getting used to me living two blocks away. He said no one told him wishing on a falling star doubled the fallout."

"That's a good one." Drake closed the truck door. "I'll keep an eye out for you when you return."

Caleb waved and drove off. Drake stomped his feet as he reached the entrance. Having family around was important. Having people who cared about you and loved you mattered too. He hoped Sara was ready to hear what his heart needed to say Christmas morning.

Drake entered the community center. Rows of tables and chairs formed a square around the center of the room. Midway through the room, a makeshift bandstand sat holding a microphone, a DJ set up and musical instruments. He continued across the room until he reached the makeshift coatroom. Three long coatracks with numbered hangers on them filled the area. Sara stood behind the counter. Two large boxes sat on the counter.

"Good evening, sir. Welcome to Peyton Corner's Fund Raiser Dinner and Dance. May I take your jacket?" Sara winked and blew him a kiss as he reached the counter.

"Well, my date might not like me flirting. You can take my jacket but not sure I can take that kiss." Drake stuffed his watch cap in his jacket pocket and tossed the jacket on the counter. "Maybe I will take that kiss."

He puckered his lips and leaned toward Sara. She brushed her lips across his cheek.

"I believe, sir, your date approves of that kiss. Now here's your number and go see Michael for your inside duty station assignment." Sara held out a numbered card to Drake.

Drake pocketed the card, blew Sara a kiss and walked over to where Michael stood. "Reporting for duty. Where you got me stationed?"

"Front door with Nelson, selling tickets and helping Lindsay with collecting payment. Some folks prepaid. Nelson has that list. Lindsay is handling receipts and credit card transactions." Michael held out two boxes. "Red tickets prepaid. Green tickets pay now. The blue tickets are for the baked goods auction. Each ticket is five dollars."

Drake nodded. "Got it. Come on, Nelson. Let's get set up."

Nelson hesitated. "Got one question, Michael. When do we eat?"

"Serving starts at 7:30. Most folks should arrive between 6:30 and 7. You can eat when the serving starts. Make sure one of you covers the entrance up till about 8ish. Anyone who arrives after that pays half price for the dance and the baked goods auction." Michael patted Nelson's shoulder. "Lindsay says Maria made her special Lasagna Italiano. Enjoy!"

Nelson walked away. Drake turned to Michael. "Think they're next to jump the broom?"

"Don't know. Maria asked Lindsay several times if Nelson was attending tonight." Michael shrugged. "Maybe you and Sara are next."

Drake held up his hand. "Hush. That is personal if such talk happens."

Michael chuckled, nodding. "Yeah, that was supposed to happen with Frank and Elly. The whole station knew before they did. We'll see what happens."

"Yeah, right. I've got door duty. Talk to you later, Michael." Drake walked away clutching the cash and ticket boxes with one hand and reaching into his pocket with his other. Would Sara accept part of his Christmas present tonight?

CHAPTER TWENTY-ONE

Three hours later

Lindsay pulled out the chair next to Drake. "Michael is bringing over our dinner. Sara is waiting for you next to the main serving table. Enjoy your meal."

"Thanks, Lindsay. You and Michael enjoy yours." Drake stood up, stretched and moved away from the table. His stomach growled and gurgled, protesting its emptiness. He counted the number of empty chairs as he made his way through the dining area. They'd set up for over two hundred attendees. Almost every chair was filled, including the children's tables. Nelson's initial tally of the receipts indicated they'd raised five thousand dollars in the first half-hour. Nelson's recent tally put the total at forty-five thousand dollars. Donations from the local businesses plus the churches' fundraising, the fundraiser had surpassed its goal. They raised close to a hundred thousand dollars. With the amount of the state grant plus the federal one, the urgent care center and new fire station was financially ready to break ground.

Drake slipped his arm around Sara's waist and hugged her to him. "Ready for dinner, sexy?"

Sara faced him. "Good thing I knew it was you. Hate to have tossed you onto the cake table. Too many good-looking cakes to waste them that way."

Drake snickered. "Well, I am not much of a cake eater. I don't think my figure would look good in it either."

"True. You look better—naked and sprawled in bed." Sara started to move away.

Drake tightened his hold on her. "Are you flirting with me?"

"Nah, I'm propositioning you. Gonna take me up on it when we get home?" Sara looped her arms around his neck.

"Hmm, I'll think about it." Drake kissed Sara's cheek. "Right now, I want dinner. Barbecue pork, salad, and Lindsay said something about her molasses brown sugar twice baked beans. Then maybe a small piece of your cake if I win the auction."

"Our plates and drinks are on the table over there." Sara pointed toward the corner where a small table with two chairs was.

"Reserved us a private spot. Nice." Drake took Sara's hand and started toward the table.

"It was the only spot that hadn't sold. Lindsay told Michael to save it for someone special. I didn't ask why."

Drake pulled out the chair closest to him as he reached the table. "Michael asked who would sit here so close to the coatroom and the kids' area. I said Sara and I. Kids will be busy visiting Santa. The coats are within eyesight. Don't need much babysitting."

Sara sat down. "True. It also keeps us out of the crowd. No need to spend dinner trying to socialize and gulp food."

Drake spread his napkin on his lap. He picked up his glass, sniffed and grinned. "Ginger ale. Awesome!"

"Yes, the local brewery donated a hundred cases. Joe said it was the most requested beverage after Peyton Corner's winery's rose and blush wines." Sara smoothed her napkin on her lap, picked up her glass, and touched it to his. "Here's to holidays, a successful fundraiser, and to us."

"To us, good food, a successful event, and the holidays." Drake pointed at his plate. "Here's to another wonderful meal together."

"Good food. Great company." Sara pointed to the bread plate sitting between them. "Mama Lucia sent a separate batch of her cinnamon yeast rolls just for you."

Drake picked up a roll, held it close to his nose, and inhaled. Cinnamon, brown sugar and a bit of nutmeg tantalized him. He tore the roll in several pieces, laid them on top of the shredded pork and mixed them together. "Tangy, hot, and sweet all together. Here's to an awesome meal."

Sara broke a piece off her roll and mixed it with her shredded pork. She forked part of the mix into her mouth. Bursts of sugar, followed by the heat of the jalapeno juice, worked their way across her taste buds as she chewed. Here and there, she caught hints of nutmeg and cinnamon. She picked up her glass and drank. "Wow, that is good. Your idea or Mama Lucia's?"

Drake wiped his mouth. "Both. I taught her about yeast rolls. She taught me about using leftover pizza dough to make dessert."

"Something tells me, I need to get you into my kitchen more often." Sara went back to eating.

"That sounds like a possibility." Drake grinned, winked and continued eating.

Forty minutes passed as the attendees got seconds and thirds from the main food tables. As a food table emptied, servers and staff from the station cleared the tables and moved them up against the wall.

Drake scooted his chair closer to Sara on his second return to their table. "Music and dancing are starting soon. Do you want anything else from the buffet?"

"No, thank you. " Sara held up the last of the rolls. "This is my dessert. Those baked goods look delicious. I'm not bidding."

"Me either. Lindsay's half-n-half cupcakes are good. One is enough for me." Drake wiped his hands on his napkin. "Want more to drink?"

"Please. Bottle of water." Sara stood and stacked their plates. "I'll help with busing the tables and meet you back here in a few."

Drake nodded and rose. "I'll be right back with a couple bottles of water."

Sara placed their recyclables and trash in the appropriate bins. She finished wiping off the table as Drake returned. He set both bottles on the table. "Okay. As soon as cleanup is done and the food trucks packed up, Michael says we're off event duty."

"And?" Sara asked, opening one of the bottles.

"Music, dancing and holding you close." Drake opened the other bottle and drank a third of it. "Be back soon."

The attendees and the station crew cleared away the rest of the tables. Chairs were set up along the sidewalls for those who wanted to sit rather than dance. At the center of the back wall, two spotlights shined down on a keyboard, a set of drums, two guitars and a microphone.

Michael stepped up to the microphone. "Folks, I want to thank you all for attending. We crushed our hundred thousand dollar goal. Tonight with your help, we raise two hundred thousand dollars. Way to go, Peyton Corners!"

Applause and cheers broke out. As the noise diminished, four musicians took the stage. Michael shook the hand of the band member closest to him. "Ladies and gentleman, without further ado, here's Peyton Corners' own Blue Ridge Jazz."

The opening chords of Don't Let My Heart Bail began. The lights dimmed until only the microphone stood out. A shadow moved toward the microphone. A familiar baritone voice sang.

"Twice my heart threatened to bail

I know better now

Gotta listen to my heart

Hear the message it sends

Gotta know and understand

Falling for you

Yes I am, my dear

I got a feeling this time

My heart isn't going to bail

I'm not letting my heart bail

I know I love you

'Cuz I've fallen for you."

As the light brightened, Drake sang louder, repeating the last stanza. The melody repeated once and faded as Drake sang the last two lines, "I know I love you 'cuz I've fallen for you." The stage went dark. Applause roared and continued as Blue Ridge Jazz started another song.

Several couples moved on to the dance floor. Drake made his way over to where Sara sat, clutching her water bottle. He held out one hand. "For some, the holidays signify change. A renewal, a fresh start, or even an end. Will you help me make a fresh start? Renew my faith in love and joy? End my lonely solo existence?"

Sara laid the empty bottle on the table, stood, and took Drake's hand. "Yes. Yes. Yes. I know I've fallen for you because I love you too."

Drake pulled Sara tightly to him, brushed his lips over hers, and whispered, "Let's go home where we can show each other what loving and falling for you means."

EPILOGUE

Christmas Morning-Two Days Later

C Sara snuggled closer to Drake. He slipped his arm around her waist, hugging her to him, his hot breath warming her neck. "Morning, darlin'. Sleep well?"

Sara slid her hand down until her fingers entwined with Drake's. "Yes, awesomely well. You?"

"Best sleep I've had in a long time. Sated, blissed out, and . ..I'll leave the rest to your imagination." Drake nipped her neck.

"I was right there too. Memories are better than imagination. Though imagination can liven things up for the next time." Sara pulled her hand away from Drake's. She sat up, tucking the blankets under her arms.

Drake sat up next to her, yawning as he stretched. "Yes, you minx, your imagination can heat things up quite a bit."

Sara ducked her head, feeling warmth creeping up her neck. She reached for the boxes on her nightstand. She laid them on the bed between Drake and her. "Can we open presents now? McGee is enjoying his."

Two heads popped up in the crate. McGee and his companion yawned, yipped, and snuggled deeper into their new bed and blankets. Cherish's brownish-red fur stood out as she curled tighter to McGee. The four-month-old pup had stolen both her and Drake's hearts from the moment they'd seen her picture. Bringing her home on Christmas Eve had been a surprise present from Lindsay and Michael.

"Sure, we can open presents." Drake laid his two wrapped boxes next to Sara's. "Who goes first?"

"I will." Sara grinned, reaching for the small box closest to her. Drake laid his hand on hers. "The bigger one first, please. They go together."

Sara looked at him quizzically. "Okay. Why don't you open one of mine first then?"

"Okay. I choose the Santa paper one." Drake picked up the eight by ten-sized package. He ripped open the paper. The backside of a frame came into view. He flipped the frame over and grinned. The framed picture was from the afternoon he and McGee had sacked out in his hammock sleeping side-by-side. "This is awesome. Thank you, sweetie. Go ahead and open yours."

Sara tore open the paper on the larger package. Two envelopes fell out. She glanced at him as she turned over one of the envelopes. "Why would you be giving me this?"

"I'll explain after you open the envelope."

Sara tore the envelope open and unfolded the paper inside. Her hand shook as she looked up. "I got the job?"

"Sweetie, you're credentials, referrals and work sample stood out. Dr. Walston told Michael and me that your passion and commitment to health care and sexual education made you the best candidate." Drake cupped her chin and kissed her. "Assistant Director of Marketing and Education. Congratulations."

"And the second envelope?" Sara put the paper she held back in the first envelope.

"Why don't I open the second one from you?" Drake grinned. "Yes, I am prolonging your waiting."

"Go ahead. I can wait." Sara handed him the gift.

Drake ripped open the paper. "When did you find time to make these?" He put on the watch cap and wrapped the matching scarf around his neck. "The colors are the same as the afghan I've got."

"I found the yarn when I was getting things together for the community center bazaar. I'd made the hat and scarf months ago with you in mind before I knew you had the afghan." Sara kissed his cheek. "I'm glad you like them."

"They're awesome. Time to open the small box." Drake handed Sara the box.

Sara untied the ribbon around the worn velveteen box. She carefully opened the box. Inside revealed a ring with amethyst and periwinkle stones. She looked up. Drake's gaze met hers. "Is this. . ." Words failed her.

Drake took the box and her hand. "My great grandfather was a jeweler. He made this ring for my great grandma's sixteenth birthday. It later became their engagement ring. My grandfather proposed to my grandmother with it. It missed my dad because he and mom eloped."

"You're..." Sara didn't say more.

"I'm proposing. Sara, will you spend the rest of your life with me? Celebrate with me our new beginnings as we joyously thrive in our mutual love and partnership?"

Sara nodded. "Yes, I'll do this. I'll marry you. I love you."

Drake let go of her hand, took the ring out of the box and placed it on her finger. "Good 'cuz the other envelope needs opening."

Sara tore open the envelope. Two tickets fell out. She picked one up, glanced at it and at Drake. Her mouth opened. No words came out.

Drake kissed her cheek. "How about getting married in the place you've always wanted to visit? Hawaii?"

Sara dropped the ticket, flung her arms around Drake's neck. Happy tears trickled down her cheek. Who knew falling for their next-door neighbor would bring each of them such a wealth of happiness and love.

THE END

Don't miss out!

Visit the website below and you can sign up to receive emails whenever Solara Gordon publishes a new book. There's no charge and no obligation.

https://books2read.com/r/B-A-RAUJ-RGSRB

BOOKS 2 READ

Connecting independent readers to independent writers.

Also by Solara Gordon

Cascade Bay
Love Reborn

Peyton Corners
Falling for You

Standalone
A Heart's Desire
To Love You Again
To Love You Again

Watch for more at https://solaragordon.com/.

About the Author

Solara loves and lives with her partner of 21 years in the Metro DC area. What started out as a bi-coastal romance soon settled on one coast.

A vivid imagination keeps her busy creating her next fascinating romance. She enjoys creating unique characters and watching their journeys unfold. "Love freely given multiplies and will return endlessly" is a key aspect of her stories. Add in alternative lifestyles and her love for the paranormal, and the uncommon becomes the norm in many of her stories.

Her day job in the financial services industry pays the bills while she pens her erotic tales.

Read more at https://solaragordon.com/.

www.ingramcontent.com/pod-product-compliance
Lightning Source LLC
Chambersburg PA
CBHW030526260626
47157CB00005B/1895